MILLI

by

Alexandra Iff

Love is the only energy in the universe that man has not learned to drive at will.

Albert Einstein

Table of Contents

Forty Years Ago

Shh… Quiet.

Don't let them hear you. Or else they'll come.

I don't want them to come. This is my room. My space.

A doll's house that I've been living in since they brought me here. No windows though. Just a small dog flap at the bottom, closed with a latch from outside.

But still, it's mine.

It's the only thing I have.

Why? Trust me, knowledge is not power, no matter what everyone says.

CHAPTER 1

"No way," I stomp my foot.

"Lizzie, honey, please, try to understand."

"Dad, I'm sorry for mom, I really am. But I'm not going to London!!"

"One of us has to go to London for the execution of your grandmamma's will. Now that the police are treating her death as suspicious, it can't be postponed, you must go."

"Why me, then? And why now? You kept me on a short leash for so long and now, suddenly, I can go by myself all the way to London?! Uh-uh!"

"Why? Because you've stopped studying, you're not working, and really, Lizzie, we need you to do something for us. You cannot just stay in your room and do nothing all day and night."

"What about mom's other relatives? Why can't they go?"

"What other relatives? You act as if you're not part of this family anymore. Your mom is an only child, you know that. And with her health deteriorating drastically, we can't expect her to fly to London. She's not coping well," he looks towards the bedroom, where mom has been ever since she heard the news of her mother falling down the stairs and dying in her house in London, England.

"But dad…."

"You and your grandmamma had a special bond, and I know she would have wanted you to go. You, and nobody else."

"Don't give me that bull crap, dad. She's not my real grandmother! Let me ask you this, how would they let a child execute her will? I'm not even twenty-one yet."

"Your mother has given you a power of attorney. That's all you need. Once you get

4

there, you'll need to call grandmamma's solicitors and they'll do the rest."

"See? I don't have a clue what you're talking about. Solicitors??"

"It's an English word for lawyers. Your job will be to record every item in her house, and then, with their help, get rid of it, sell it. The probate lawyer who agreed to oversee all this at such short notice, some big shot from London, umm, he's called Leopold Fitzgerald, said this has to be done as soon as possible. In the letter to your mother he noted the only day and time he could do it. And he said if your mother is not available, you must go in her place. If you don't, your grandfather would be covering it solely."

"There you go! That's perfect!"

"It's not. I've been there and I think there's a lot of valuable stuff in grandmamma's house. If you don't go, your grandfather would take it all. Honey, you know how much we need the money right now."

My grandfather divorced grandmamma before I was born, and I've never really spoken to him. The only time I saw him was when me and dad took a detour from France, and flew to London to surprise grandmamma before heading back home to Boston. He was visiting her at the time and all he did, after the introduction, was disturbingly stare at me. He didn't even say hello. No hugging or kissing, or any of those normal things grandparents do. I call him Edwin, just like my mother calls him, by his name. Mom had always hated him, don't know why though. They haven't spoken to each other for many, many years.

"Shit, dad, I'm not going on this guilt trip. I don't want it! Mom should go. She would know more than me anyway."

"Your mother needs to stay here, she's sick. But she did make an inventory of the items in grandmamma's house as much as she could remember. You will go by that list."

"And make sure you use Leopold Fitzgerald to your advantage. That's crucial. Do not miss that appointment. He seems like a very busy man. Be there before the time is up, and more importantly, be ready."

"What about my job search, dad?"

"Really? You are pulling out that card? Tell me, Lizzie, how many jobs did you apply for in the last six months? Or better yet, tell me what you have been doing all this time? Maybe it will help me understand."

I don't answer him. He's right. Bull crap. Ever since they told me I'm adopted, my life as I knew it, ceased to exist. Why did they have to tell me? I was perfectly happy living a lie. *A lie that I loved.* I was finally going to college after years of being home-schooled, getting good grades, meeting friends for the first time since I can remember. And for a short while, I even had a boyfriend.

The moment mom went to the hospital, everything that could go wrong for me, did. The doctors said they must operate urgently or she'll die. Was she afraid she'd die without telling me? All I remember is a rainy day, and me sitting down on her hospital bed, holding her hand.

Dad had his hand on my shoulder.

"Lizzie," mom couldn't finish the sentence, she had tears rolling down her cheeks, and she was gasping for air. Dad got her asthma inhaler and gave it to her. Every single illness that was out there, mom had it.

While repeating in my head the mantra *'Please don't die'* I genuinely thought that she would. Why else would I be summoned to her bed? I had searing pain in my stomach, my heart was breaking in two, I'd give my life in an instant just so she could live. She…she's my mom. My father was standing by my side, tears streamed down his cheeks, too.

"My baby girl. I want you to know something," she was crying as she was talking. I should have been the one crying, but my eyes were dry. On the inside, I was tearing up.

"There's something I must tell you," she paused her heavy breathing. "You… You are adopted. I am not your mother."

The next moment I remember is being completely deaf. My dad's lips were moving but I couldn't hear anything. My face contorted in denial, I shook my head, I wanted to run away from there but my father's strong hands kept me in place. I had to stay, and absorb her guilt, her fabricated story, and their lies.

For a tiny moment that day, a part of me hoped that she'd told me that she was dying.

I'm the worst daughter anyone could ever wish for. No wonder I was given up for adoption.

She must have wanted me to be miserable, just like she is, and has been all her life. *I wasn't ready for the truth.* And now they expect me to sort out the will for grandmamma, who is not my real grandmamma anymore?

"Lizzie, come back with the money. You are your mother's last hope."

Guilt trip. That's how they are managing me these days. If you don't do this, your mom will die. If you do this, your mom will die. My 'adoptive' mother has been suffering from depression all her life. I know what she is like. But now that she is in a late stage of breast cancer, if we don't find the money soon, she'll certainly die.

And grandmamma, I hate that I miss her so much.

I turn around in frustration and stomp back to my room.

I grab my pink teddy, press it tight against my chest and collapse on my bed. The

9

instant surge of tears blurs my sight. Grandmamma and I were close. True, I've seen her only once in my life, on my short visit to London, but that doesn't mean I didn't know her. We talked on the phone nearly every day, without mom knowing, of course. Why couldn't she stay alive, forever? You were the anchor in my life, grandmamma. I never got to tell you that. The lump in my throat is getting bigger as silent tears run down my cheeks. I sniffle.

When I was drowning in sorrow, falling apart, wondering what was so wrong with me that my birth mother would give me away, her words meant so much. *Lizzie, sometimes life is tough. But you must ignore the pain, and smile. Remember, You create your own happiness.* She was the best grandmamma anyone could ever wish for. Real or not real.

My dad knocks on my bedroom door, and enters. I don't flinch, he's seen me cry too many times.

"I'm sorry Lizzie, it's a tough time for everyone. I know you're suffering, too. Here," he passes me a black leather folder. A stack of documents can be seen protruding at the corners. "You have all the information in there. Keep it safe. Perhaps read through it on the flight."

"When am I going?" I wipe the tears rolling down my cheek.

"Tomorrow morning. I got you a round trip ticket, Boston to London, departing at eight am."

"For how long?"

"A week."

Dad leaves my bedroom in his dejected state. He hasn't been feeling good either, but he's holding strong, for mom. Mom has had ups and downs throughout the years, always blaming her parents for whatever happened and is happening to her. She'd been battling anxiety and depression even before she's met my dad. Poor dad, he's been trying all his life to help her.

And now that it's my turn to grow up and live, I find it hard not to blame my parents. How could they not tell me for so long that I'm adopted? Grandmamma was only preparing me for the inevitable truth that was going to come out sooner or later.

We make our own destiny, she'd say. We grow up. We forgive. We move on. It's easier on the heart.

I swing with my arm and throw my pink teddy at the corner of my room as I start sobbing uncontrollably. *I hate my life!*

The next morning, at precisely six o'clock, I'm dropped off at Logan International Airport.

My dad doesn't waste any time with me. I also know he's tired, and on top of that he has to work two shifts at the Café today. Damn him, I hate that I feel sorry for him. He hugs me and kisses me on the forehead.

"Whatever happens, just know that you did your best. And that we love you no matter what," there is defeat in his voice that I'm not familiar with.

"What do you mean? That I can't do this?" His comment befuddles me.

"Be careful Lizzie, that's all. Have a safe trip."

I gaze at him walking away for about a second or two, and I, too, don't wait any longer. I turn around and head for the check in desks.

After a quick check in, I go through security. The security guard checks my passport, asks for my name while looking at me, and then glances at the photo in my passport again.

Once on the other side, I locate my gate, thirteen, and I hurry in that direction. I can't wait to get this over and done with.

Ten minutes later, after paced walking and shoulder bumping with hundreds of other people, I find a space on a bench in front of a busy coffee kiosk, and I sit down, waiting for 'Gate 13' to open.

I pull out of my bag the folder with the documents, and start reading, there's a lot of information that's foreign to me. Our American English and the British English sound different, or at least read different. Especially when there's lots of legal jargon involved. The only thing I understand is mom's note. In a small notebook she's put down the names of the items I would find at grandmamma's house, one by one, with a small hand drawn picture next to them.

Funny how I recall everything that's noted down. For the one time I visited grandmamma's house, I vividly remember her house being a trove of magnificent treasures and some, very old items. Mostly furniture but she'd also have the odd first edition books. She liked that stuff. The musty smell I encountered by opening some of her old credenzas and cabinets always remind me of that time in London, and her house.

I place the notebook aside, and flip the pages up to Fitzgerald Solicitors. The stationery that's written on seems more expensive than my laptop. All these embossed letters, stamps and foundation names aligned at the bottom. Supporters of Fitzgerald Solicitors. The letter has my name on it, with a date from two weeks ago. This gets me annoyed. Mom and dad told them I'd be the one going.

To Eliza Milli Cruz, Monday, ten o'clock in the morning, St. Paul's Churchyard, City of London. On the second page there is a photograph of ten people posing in front of a lavish glass building. They're all wearing impeccable suits, and, over their wrinkly old skin, trained smiles on their faces. Behind them, in large letters engraved on the glass, it reads Fitzgerald Solicitors. At least I know where I'll be going to on Monday.

I close the folder and put it aside. I still have time before the gate opens, and I already feel anxious. I lift my gaze to the people around me to see who I'd be flying with. We were never designed to fly like birds and of course, whenever I get into a "flying machine" I'm confronting my deepest fears. Naturally, I need to see if the people flying with me are composed and calm, because finding myself way up in the sky, sealed in a machine with my weak heart beating in my ears for eight hours, I'd definitely go crazy.

A few people give me a fake smile, confirming my dread that I'm on my own on this flight. I radiate fear and nobody wants to come near me. I continue to observe around the room when I come across an intensive stare. No fake smile or anything. He's standing on the other side of the gate, leaning on a pillar, and glaring at me unnervingly. Blond, messy hair, blue eyes, two day stubble. I blush instantly. I glance aside, and a few seconds later, back at him just to see if it's me he's looking at, but he hasn't flinched, or changed the intensity of his stare. Then, just as I feel my stomach churning and the pull from his eyes become hypnotic, he looks away, turning his back on me.

I blink a few times, I need a moment to compose myself. *Men want only one thing,* mom says. As long as I keep that in mind, I'll be fine.

The deep voice coming from his direction makes me look up again. It's him. He excuses himself while he picks up his bag and, standing up straight, he starts walking towards me. I glance down, at my feet and, five seconds later I feel an overbearing presence next to me, and his eyes burning a hole on my skin. I wish my heart would stop beating so fast. *He may hear it.*

I look up coolly, and reminding myself of my mom's words, my eyes narrow a little. He picked the wrong girl to mess with. I may have been home-schooled and a sweet girl at home, but I learned how to be tough in the past six months. Or at least, how to act tough.

"Eliza Cruz?"

"M-maybe."

"Eliza Milli Cruz?" He repeats my name louder, his eyes inquisitively looking at me.

I'm caught off guard by his presence, his scent and his all-encompassing existence. So I decide to stand up tersely, and seeing how tall he is, I straighten more. His worn leather jacket and stubble on his face are… are too close to me.

"Yes. That's me. She is I. I am her. Ahem."

"You are her, huh? Are you travelling overseas today?"

"I-I am."

"Do you have your passport with you, gorgeous?"

"My passport?" *Why does he want my passport?* I'm staring at him while with my hand I dig into my handbag checking if I have it. But I can't find it. I panic; I cannot travel abroad if I don't have my passport. "I... I don't have it. I must have dropped it when I was walking down to the gate," I look around me baffled, searching for it on the floor. *Now is not a good time to lose my passport.*

I glance back at him again, but now I see him holding a passport in his hand and shaking his head at me like I'm an irresponsible child.

"Give me that!" I quickly snatch it from his hand, check that it's mine and tuck it safely inside my bag.

"There's no need for aggression, Miss Cruz."

"You should have handed me my passport the moment you saw me!" I press my index finger into his iron clad chest hoping to push him back a little. I fail miserably. He's a wall of hard muscle, tall, with broad shoulders. Powerful thighs under his low waist jeans, and damn cool brown, ankle boots. "What? You didn't think I'd do that?"

"Do what, beautiful?" He locks eyes with me, calm, and clear blue. Taunting me again.

"Look, asshole," I slam my open palms against his chest. "Whoever you are, I don't need you!"

In a flash he grabs my left wrist and twists me around so fast that before I know I'm slammed on the wall, my twisted arm between us, and his body pressing mine firmly against the hard and cold surface. I have never been touched by someone's full body length before. I can actually feel everything through my skirt and sweatshirt. With my face pressed flat on the wall, I notice the people staring at me, and I hear them gasping in shock, some looking around for help.

"Watch where you put those pretty hands of yours next time," he growls in my ear.

"It's okay everyone, I'm an FBI agent," theatrically he pulls an identification card out of his pocket and waves it around.

"What has she done?" I hear someone ask.

"I was showing her how easy it would be to overpower someone her size," he replies.

"Yeah, yeah," I hear people agreeing.

"You look nothing like your picture," he says softly.

"Fuck you!" I huff quietly between my teeth.

CHAPTER 2

He takes a step back, releasing my arm. I'm sure he's covertly enjoying the admirable glances he gets from everyone around. A powerful agent, ruthless and cunning, probably doing the dirtiest work the agency has to offer, pinned a girl on the wall. What kind of person does that to a girl?

"You should look after your passport better. Next time you won't be so lucky," he checks my wrist and discreetly massages it, hoping to alleviate the pain he caused.

I abruptly withdraw my hand from his and look at him, the few strands of sandy hair that have fallen over his forehead are giving him a rugged model-like look, but that's more of a reason why I hate him right now. He is too handsome for me to think straight. Plus, he touched my body. Is that allowed?

Surely someone would have said something if he was touching me inappropriately.

"You consider that, what you just did, lucky for me? You're a bully as far as I'm concerned," I scoff.

He stares at me for a few moments, enough for me to decide that his cold blue stare makes me doubt everything I've ever known about the male species. As if he read my mind, without flinching he pulls his ID out of his pocket, and flips it open in front of me. Like he has done it hundreds of times before. I glance at it, and read the name and job title a few times in my head while my mind is someplace else – the way he observes my face up close. Sean O'Connell.

"Beautiful or not, when you mess with the FBI, you get what you deserve."

"Please save me the bullshit. The FBI shouldn't be intimidating."

"You saw me looking at you earlier I take it."

"Everyone did. It was creepy."

"Good. You should look out for creeps."

"Why, when I already found one?"

A smirk appears on his face, and his heavenly blue eyes change into a few shades darker. "Are you always this feisty when you're nervous?"

"I-I'm not nervous at all."

"Then I'd be careful what I'm saying if I was you."

"Or what? You'd twist my arm and slam me against a wall at your first chance?" I'm angry with him, and yet, flustered.

"Maybe," he smiles. Then he picks up his bag and walks away into the line of a busy café. I'm left standing by myself, feeling stupid because I let him talk to me. *Get to me.*

I go back to the bench where I was earlier, and sit down. I turn my face in the direction opposite of where he is. Perhaps I should have said thank you.

"Going to London, too?"

A young woman, oblivious to what just happened, has sat down next to me.

I nod, "It looks like it's going to be a long flight."

"Not for me. I'll be reading. The flight should take me about two books." She grins, pointing to her Kindle.

"I'll try to get some sleep."

"Have you been there before?"

"Yes. My mom is from England."

Although if it wasn't for my father, I'd never go there. Mom would never take me to England. She hates it.

"You?"

"My first time. I'm so excited. My cousin, Mateo, got a job at the US Embassy in London. He's been there for a few years already and he has finally invited me to visit. He says I'm going to love it. And unless he's working, he'd take me everywhere in London. I'm Olivia by the way."

"Eliza."

"Nice to meet you, Eliza."

I smile and notice her slightly pulling back, trying to avoid a man marching brusquely past us. Seeing him from behind and the way he paces forth, he reminds me of a young James Bond, trying to escape a room full of adversaries. He has a black flat cap on his head and is wearing a grey, well-fitted suit, perfectly tailored to his measurements. Even his shiny black shoes are perfect.

Just as I become aware of his expensive scent lingering in the air, I feel his leaden bag pulled across my leg, bashing straight into my knee, and I cry out in pain.

A skirt for the flight was not the best idea. After the close contact I had with the FBI I feel more than ever exposed. I check my knee and see a small cut across it, a drop of blood rolling down. I glance at the man who's now stopped, and is looking baffled at us.

"Is everything all right?"

The man glances at my knee as I'm holding it, and then comes closer, unexpectedly kneeling down in front of me. He has a smooth, spade shaped dark beard and defined cheekbones, and as he's looking directly at my eyes, he extends a big, strong hand, exposing golden cufflinks that bear initials I cannot read properly.

"I sincerely apologize. I didn't mean to hurt you in any way," he takes my hand in his, locking me with his eyes and, now openly observing my lips, and my face. His hair is meticulously groomed, his tourmaline-black eyes could easily serve me as a talisman of protection, but he is too daring, he's standing in my personal space, something I'm not too keen on.

"It's okay. I'm fine," I awkwardly pull my hand out of his.

"You are bleeding, and it could get infected," the man points to my knee and the drawn blood on top of it.

"It's only a scratch."

Dammit. Blood is a bad sign. *I hate flying.*

"Please, allow me to help you."

"Seriously, I'm okay."

"But-,"

"I said I'm okay!" All of a sudden I yell, and everyone turn their heads in my direction. My eyebrows knit in anger. "Leave me alone, dammit."

"I'm sorry, I didn't mean...-" he stands up and with a frown on his face, retreats towards the gate like a wounded soldier.

Olivia is looking wide-eyed at me, probably shocked at my sudden outburst of emotion.

"What can I say? Flying makes me nervous," I throw my hands in the air.

I should not apologize for my behavior. To anyone.

Soon the gate opens, and everyone is ready to board the plane. The line forms and ends just about where we are. I stand up, we all do, and slowly, one by one we line up to get inside. At the entrance of the plane I'm met by the whole cabin crew smiling at me, to which I reciprocate aptly, and as I walk down the aisle and up to my seat, I realize that someone is already sitting in it.

The flight attendant standing behind me has somehow read the boarding pass in my hand. She taps my shoulder quietly. "The last row is empty, Miss Cruz. Feel free to use it."

I smile at her relieved, finally one person on my side in this godforsaken airplane. I may be okay after all. I continue through the narrow aisle, avoiding the stares from everyone that have already settled down, and finally reach that last empty row.

Before I sit down I set on making myself comfortable; I take my sweatshirt off and place it in the overhead compartment. Then I get inside between the seats, and sit down by the window. Now, I'm ready to face my demise. Or whatever this flight will turn out to be.

With me being the last passenger on board, I hear the flight attendant already on the loud speaker, telling us what to do in an emergency. The silence in the plane means everyone is looking at her with great attention. I don't, I've flown a few times before. I know what it's about, and I couldn't care less. My fear of flying is taking over. I'm leaned back in my tiny seat, my arms crossed over my chest and my eyes closed. Stubbornly hoping to fall asleep.

A few minutes later I hear another flight attendant talking to me.

"Excuse me, Miss, please could you open the shutter on the window?"

Reluctantly I open the window shutter, only because I know they won't budge, and I cross my arms again.

"Please fasten your seatbelts, the plane is about to take off," the flight attendant on the speakers continues.

I don't move. Nervous or not nervous, when did it ever made any difference if you are wearing a seatbelt in an airplane?

"Please, Miss, fasten your seatbelt."

Dammit, they've seen me. If I pretend I'm asleep they might leave me alone.

"Miss? Miss Cruz?"

"Why don't you check on the other passengers, I got this."

He's sitting next to me? This row was empty! *What does he want?* The seats are small, the space confined, and he's... he's so handsome. I don't move; I'm anxiously expecting him to say something while hoping he'd believe I'm asleep, but the silence is overbearing, and I'm intimidated again.

"There is a flashing sign above your head, beautiful," Sean O'Connell's voice is too calm.

I keep my eyes closed. I can't deal with him and flying at the same time.

The next moment I hear him fiddling with something and then, distressingly, I sense his hands grazing my thighs. I open my eyes in panic just when he locks my seatbelt and pulls the end tight, making me gasp. The jolt makes my body pull back into the seat, and I grip the arm rests.

Our eyes lock, and I'm not sure what's happening. The fact that he is so uncomfortably close makes me stop breathing. There's no space to pull back so I hold my breath while with my hands I frantically search for the buckle to set myself free.

His hot palm on my skin short circuits my body on fire.

"Tighter?"

"N-no… That's good," I whisper.

I tilt my head back on the seat, close my eyes and exhale quietly. I need to cool off. I just about start breathing when something, gently, starts rubbing my left breast through the thin material of my t-shirt.

"Hell, no!"

I dig in my nails into whatever is touching me and open my eyes. It's the back of his upper arm, he's searching for his seatbelt that's lost somewhere between our seats. He turns around, and unfortunately for me, realizes what's happening. *Could anyone actually feel something with the back of their arm?* The way he looks at me, I think he has.

"Do that one more time - FBI or not -you'll be sorry. I mean it," I growl at him, partly embarrassed but mostly annoyed at my presumption, and the fact that I'm losing my mind because of this damned flight.

"The flight will be over in no time, try to think about something else if you can," he smirks and moves one seat away, thankfully.

"Ugh. I hate flying," I murmur to myself.

"I'm Sean. Sean O'Connell, nice to meet you," he reaches his hand out to me.

The pilots suddenly turn on the engines, the noise rapidly saturates the plane, and my head too, making me grab the armrest firmly, and tilt my head back. Who am I fooling? My body is vibrating in fear. Taking off and descending make my belly all woozy. I open my eyes a few seconds later and see him observing me calmly, his eyes traveling all over my face. His hand is still out, waiting on me to take it.

"Eliza Cruz, but you know that already," I shake his hand quickly and go back to holding the armrest firmly.

My mom taught me a lot about men. They are not to mess with. They are evil, and they will use me. *I hate mom.* Why was she married, then? So many contradictions, and yet, I wasn't allowed to ask any questions.

Look after your innocence, never let men use you. Remember, you are in charge. Really? I'm in charge? When have I ever been in charge?

"Stop thinking about the flight, Eliza."

My heartbeat is drumming like crazy and all I want is some peace in my head. Everything is fusing together, it's deafening.

"Your fear of flying is unreasonable."

"Well, what are you going to do about it?" I yell over the noise.

The engines being to roar and the plane barrels down the runway, accelerating faster and faster as Sean unbuckles his seatbelt, moves into the seat next to me and buckles himself again. Just as the noise becomes ear-splitting and the plane ascends, Sean grabs my wrists in one hand and holds me tight as suddenly I find myself fighting against him. *What the hell?* There is no struggle on his part, he's stronger than me by far. With the other hand he grabs my chin and forcefully pulls me to him, leaving a kiss on my lips so potent, and brutal, it sucks the air out of my lungs completely. And when he parts my lips and inserts his tongue inside my mouth, deep, I think he consumes everything that I am. Everything that I stand for. Every molecule in my body that fought against having any connection with men, it melts away.

Just as the noise subdues the kiss dies too, he pulls back, but is still within the proximity of my heartbeat. His eyes are glued on my lips, now glossy from our kiss. "Just as I thought, perfect," and slowly, they rise up to my eyes. Quickly, he blinks, clearing his throat, and he pulls back. "Kissing relieves tension, reduces negative energy and produces a sense of well-being," I feel the rush of air coming out of his lips as he is talking.

Peaches and cream.

The snapping of his seatbelt is my wake up call. He stands up and moves back where he was sitting. "In other words, you're welcome."

Speechless, I look at him as he leans on the armrest with his elbow, his fingers gingerly stroking his lips. He's absentmindedly staring at his iPad, unashamedly ignoring what just happened.

I turn my head to the window and close my eyes, my body still going through the reverberations of the kiss. Where's my voice gone? He was right. Right now I think of many things, but the flight itself, even though we are fully airborne.

The following ten - fifteen minutes drag on forever, torture me into actively thinking of white clouds, because, I cannot think of anything else to erase my maddening thoughts. I have to get away from him. He's too much. When the light above our heads pings off, I know it's time.

"Excuse me, may I?" I half stand up, and patently wait, avoiding eye contact until he, too, stands up and makes way for me.

"Feeling better already?"

"Not really."

He stands in the aisle, waiting on me to leave my seat. Once out I turn around, hoping to get as far away from him as possible when out-of-nowhere turbulence pushes me backwards, into him, again. I gasp as his strong arm wraps around my waist, and pulls me flat against his body.

"You can't get enough of me, can you?" he teases me quietly.

Why am I so affected by him? Is it because he is with the FBI? I doubt it. He's holding me firmly as I pull away from him; I want to run away from here, from this airplane.

I quickly walk up to where the toilets are, and at the same time search for Olivia. Seeing her among the rows of people seating up front, and the empty space next to her, I meander around the seats, reaching hers.

"Hey," I give her a small nudge. She's lost in the book she's reading, unaware of anything and anyone around her. "Reading something interesting?"

"Oh, I didn't see you there. When did you sit next to me?"

"Just now."

"I thought you were going to sleep," she closes her kindle and places it in the net pocket in front of her.

"It's hard to sleep when you have people interrupting you all the time. Plus, it's daytime."

"That's why I have my kindle. Do you want a magazine or something?"

"Naah, I'm fine. If you don't mind, I'm going to sit here for the rest of the flight and hopefully, sleep."

"Sure."

Olivia picks up her kindle again as I buckle up and lean back, closing my eyes.

Shh… Quiet. Stop talking.

I don't want them to come. If they do, they'll let me out.

And the only time I'm let out is when they want to play. The latch of my dollhouse is open, my bottom is out and … and I'm theirs for the night.

Until I adjust, they said. Until I fully understand my role.

What is my role, you ask?

My stomach churns in disgust when I think about it. My palms sweat, I threw up when they told me, and I know I'll be sick now, too.

It's who I am, they said. My mother doomed me to this life.

Mothers should protect. Mothers should not rest until their offspring are safe.

Not curse. Not agree to... God forsaken deeds.

Apparently I can't change anything even if I wanted to.

Nobody can.

It's in my blood.

CHAPTER 3

Sean O'Connell has kept his distance for the rest of the flight. Anyway, it felt good sleeping next to Olivia. It felt safe. That's another reason why her and me exchanged numbers and agreed to see each other in London. I found out that her cousin Mateo lives in Chelsea, close to where grandmamma's house is. Now that grandmamma is not around, I'll be all by myself, and she could be too if her cousin, Mateo, is busy.

Standing under the Arrivals sign, Olivia and I hug goodbye when I finally get a glimpse of Sean. His eyes follow my every move from afar. He is behind us, in the distance, his bag on his shoulder, his hair ruffled. He must have been sleeping. I don't care.

He kissed me.

Olivia waves at me again and heads towards the London underground. Her cousin will be waiting for her on the Piccadilly Line platform, heading east. I'm left to ponder for a moment what should I do when I clock a man holding a card sign with my name on it "Eliza Milli Cruz". If grandmamma's lawyers sent a car to pick me up, I'm not paying a taxi, that's for sure.

"I'm Eliza Cruz," I say to the man holding the sign.

"Eliza *Milli* Cruz?" Sweating profusely, the man repeats my full name.

"Yes."

He grabs my bag from my hand, and hurries in front of me. "You better catch up, Miss," he says in a foreign accent, "I'm parked on a double yellow line, I might get a fine if we don't hurry up."

I don't have time to react, I practically run after him when I hear someone behind me call my name, in the distance. A few times. I look back, but there are too many people. Anyway, there are other Elizas in the world.

Pushing hastily through the crowd, the sweaty man reaches the exit and his car, a black Range Rover. I follow closely behind, he opens the door for me, and quickly goes at the back to place my bag in the trunk.

"Eliza!" I hear it clearly now, it's Sean calling me. What more does he want from me? *He took what he wanted.* I climb into the car and look at the crowd but the moment our eyes lock, the door is shut in front of me, and the driver is now running to start the car. Slightly confused, I move closer to the door and try to open it, but it's locked.

"What's going on?" Panicked and wide-eyed I look at Sean through the glass, and then at the man in the driver's seat.

Sean has reached me now, and as I futilely try to open the door or the window, he's the first one to understand what's happening. He attempts to open the front passenger's door of the car and when that's unsuccessful he rushes around it, towards the driver but he's too late, the car drives off with a screech and with me inside, paralyzed in terror. All of a sudden my pulse is beating in my ears, blocking out all other sounds except my breathing.

"Stop the car! Who are you?" I frenziedly punch the man who's trying to defend himself with one hand while driving. "Stop the fucking car!"

I'm going to hurt him if it's the last thing I do but I cannot stop the divide rising fast between us. And I do try, I kick it with my legs. Panicked, I look back at my last resort, in search of Sean O'Connell. He's an FBI agent, he saw the whole thing.

While a few men are running around and talking into their walkie-talkies, he's managed to take hold of a car. I see his steely eyes from afar, his white knuckles holding firmly the wheel of the black Mercedes he's in. He drives off with a screech, making everyone outside the terminal turn their heads. Last thing I see before we make a turn is him, in pursuit.

All my belongings, including my cell phone, are in the trunk! I frenziedly look around for something, anything I could either open or break the window with. What the fuck is happening? Why? *WHY?* I let out a loud shriek, hoping to get to my kidnapper, or alert anyone around the moving car but I end up hearing myself scream.

The car is driving at dangerous speed on the highway, I'm being thrashed left and right inside it but it's not long before we're driving down residential roads, coming up to red traffic lights. The grotesquely perspiring kidnapper slows down and I see him glancing in the rear view mirror, shaking his head in exasperation. Then he picks up his cell.

I look behind us and see the black Mercedes Sean is in approaching really fast down the narrow road. For a moment there is a speck of hope in my heart, but my kidnapper is quick to quash it. Before the light changes to green he speeds off between the cars that are at the junction, creating a near collision for Sean with a car from the oncoming traffic. He stops, but only for a second before reversing with a screech that make the passers-by look in fear, and zooms off after us.

My face is stuck on the rear windshield, my open palms too, shouting at Sean to come and get me as he's increasingly picking up speed and catching up with us. And then, as he finally comes by our side, I see him gesturing to me to put my seatbelt on, a few times. I hastily move away, sit on the opposite side and just as I click my seatbelt in place he accelerates, and swerves the car he's driving into the Range Rover, impacting it sideways, pushing us onto the curb. My kidnapper is furious, he's on the cell, yelling in his language what I can only describe as profanities, and after a few seconds he hurls it away, the cell landing on the dashboard and falling somewhere under the front seat. Sean doesn't flinch, as if he's done this many times before he's not giving in, he drives at the same speed with the Range Rover. Nothing fazes him. He beeps his horn, and swerves really wide this time as he slams even harder into the Range Rover, pushing us into a sidewall. The Range Rover stops, and I hear the door next to me clicking open. Enraged, the driver yells at me.

"Out! Out!"

I unlock my seatbelt and jump out as he accelerates with open door, nearly clipping me with it. Sean has also stopped. He rushes out of the car as I'm running to him. My whole body is shaking, I start crying as I throw myself into his arms.

"You're okay. Everything is fine. Shh," he soothes me with anger in his eyes, as he's watching the car getting away. "You're safe now. Nothing is going to happen to you, I promise."

Nested under his leather jacket, I'm sobbing uncontrollably. *How could I be so stupid?*

"I …I nearly got kidnapped. W-why would anyone want to kidnap me?"

"I got a good look of the license plate and his face. We'll find out soon enough, don't worry. Did you book the taxi yourself?"

"N-no. I-I presumed grandmamma's lawyers sent him," I sob.

"You mean you just got into someone's car without knowing them?"

I can't stop sobbing, it's all my fault. I'm so stupid, serves me right for being told off.

"Okay, okay. I'm sorry. Lawyers. Why lawyers?"

"I-I'm here for my grandmother's will. Her lawyers are sorting everything out."

"I see. Did she leave a lot?"

"I don't know," I sniffle, wiping my nose with my hand.

"How did she die?"

"Fell down the stairs, I think."

"Accident?"

"I don't know. My father says the police don't think so."

"They don't? And nobody had the courtesy to wait for you at the airport!?" His arms protectively tighten around my body, his hands on my waist, fingers curled around it. "Fucking bastards!"

He pulls out his cell and dials a number.

"It's me, Sean O'Connell. Yes. I'm fine, thank you. Yes, in London. Listen, I got involved in something. Possible homicide. Kidnapping. No, nobody yet, because I was here. She's American. No. No. He got away. Yes, I saw him, don't worry." He looks at me. "Bring her in?"

I shake my head, and wipe my tears. My body is still trembling from the shock.

"Please take me to my grandmother's house," I say quietly.

"Tomorrow. She's tired now, and still in shock. Dammit, Darby, you make your report then. I'll come and see you after I drop her off. Yes, I'll take her to the hospital for a checkup," he cuts the line and looks at me.

"I'm fine. I don't need a hospital. I just want to go home. Please."

He's observing me appraisingly and nods.

"Come on," he guides me into the black Mercedes he was driving and as I'm still shivering from the shock, he helps me buckle the seatbelt. Then he closes the door and walks over to his side, gets inside and buckles himself in too.

"Where to?"

"M-mulberry Walk. Um... It's in Chelsea, just off King's Road."

He types the information into the GPS screen in the car, then he looks straight at the road ahead and accelerates quickly.

My entire body is trembling. I bend forward, pull my knees up and bury my face in them. I start sobbing quietly, my shoulders shaking from the emotion.

"Eliza, you're safe with me."

"They took everything I have."

"We'll get it back, I promise. Is there someone waiting for you at the house?"

"No."

I lift my head and look at him, my eyes are bloodshot red, my nose running.

"T-thank you, Sean."

We arrive outside grandmamma's house; it looks like nobody is inside, but I didn't expect it to be any different. She's gone, and except for mom and myself, there are no other relatives that could claim a stake in it.

Except, maybe my grandfather, but I doubt he'd show his face here.

Sean parks the car in the driveway and looks through the window at it.

"It's a big house. Don't you have any friends or family who could take you in for the night?"

"I'll be fine. I have to stay, I need to record the contents in the house for Monday's meeting, and I don't have much time anyway." I unbuckle my seatbelt and leave the car, but Sean does the same. He follows me to the house, and catches up with me under the small awning.

"Are you going to the police station now?"

"I'll take the car to the police station, I'm sure the owner wants to know what happened to it. I'll

"Do you have a key?" I'm forced to look up at him as he is talking but I cannot think straight from the storm happening in the lower part of my belly.

"O-one of the neighbors has it. I-I'll take it from there."

He's regarding me with peculiar, veiled affection, deep, in the same way he did this morning. I bite my lip nervously and see his hand reaching out, and taking my jaw gently, pulling me to him. I should say no, or move back, but I'm immobile, unable to stop him. He leans down, whispering over my lips.

"You have no idea how beautiful you are, Eliza."

As my eyes close I feel his teeth nipping my lower lip. I pull away, hoping he'll release me but he's holding me firmly, stirring an unexpected moan out of my lips. That's the moment when his hand slips into my hair, and he parts my lips with his tongue, engaging in a passionate, raw dance with mine, consuming everything that I am yet again. My legs buck, my mind is blank, I cannot speak. He finishes with another nip on my lips, and a soft kiss. With my eyes closed, I'm focusing on the endorphins coursing through my body.

"Stay safe, beautiful, yeah? Until tomorrow."

Apparently, I'm a direct descendant of Marie-Dorothée de Rousse.

I don't know for sure, but *they* are certain of it.

The mistress of Marquis de Sade. The one he wrote about in his memoirs. The one he loved the most.

Yes, I too asked, who the fuck is Marquis de Sade?

Instead of answering, they made me read everything he's written.

Because how else would I know what this Gentleman's Club is all about?

My new life belongs to them.

To do anything they please with it.

For twenty years.

Marie-Dorothée de Rousset, nicknamed Milli, agreed to it.

They showed me the letter, framed in gold, hanging on the wall in the main room.

That's where my bloody, cursed, hellish entombed fate was framed.

My dearest Donatien,

How can one mortal get enough of you, the almighty? One lifetime is not enough for me. I want more, my debauched pleasure-seeking, immoral wolf. Much more!

Do you remember the night when we walked by the river and you pointed to the faint light? I saw every single shade of black in it. That was the night you taught me how to float, to live, and to die.

And so I knew there was a way.

As long as there is a female descendant of mine walking on this earth, I want you to be there to show her what I am. What I thrive on - hedonism, torture and ecstasy. A triple layer of love. A messy cake with an addictive aftertaste. To keep coming back for more.

Take her when she turns seventeen, and use her like you use me. I know what you're thinking now, old age will claim you eventually. And that's true. But my darling Donatien, people such as you are timeless.

Pass this letter to your followers, and they will make sure my wish is fulfilled.

Choose a Luminary, and set the fire burning for the generations to come.

But do not take my words lightly. My descendant should never suffer. She should be living in total ecstasy, and free will, like I do now. Twenty years is what I suggest, or until her fortieth birthday, should she survive the torment. (Ha-ha!)

Then, she should reclaim her life, as she pleases to. Of course, presented with dowry enough to last her until her death. Why?

Because my breed is not cheap, my dearest Donatien. You said so yourself.

Your little beast,

Milli

Marie-Dorothée de Rousset

October, 1782

CHAPTER 4

It appears that grandmamma has become a hoarder in the past five years. The interior in her Edwardian house is heavier and more cluttered than it was when I visited her before. The air is sticky and heavy from the old stuff she has. Even the windows are covered in gunk. I remember them being impeccably clean when I was here. Grandmamma liked to watch the road a lot, to marvel the outside world often, she'd say.

Anna, the neighbor from next door was very kind; she gave me fifty pounds for food and clothing while I sort myself out. After telling her what had happened to me, she thought I should have gone to the police, so they would start an official enquiry. Without enquiry, some other girl might get kidnapped in the same way. She made me feel guilty. I wish I'd done that.

Upstairs, in grandmamma's bedroom, I drifted away, and tried to edit everything that happened today.

Why did he kiss me? He keeps saying I'm beautiful, but maybe that's his way of getting to me. The first time was forced, but necessary. He helped me with my fear of flying. He saved me, too. So I forgave him. The second kiss was totally uncalled for.

When the thoughts about Sean O'Connell would go into remission, the horrific attack I lived through the moment I landed here was on replay in my head. All my belongings are gone, too. The documents, my laptop, my passport... My life.

Ignore the pain, and smile. You create your own happiness.

Grandmamma, it's really hard to do that when you fear for your life.

The phone ringing jolts me; I get up, and quickly head downstairs to answer it. I enter the large living room, and pick up the old-fashioned black handset.

"Hello?"

"Welcome to London, Lizzie."

"Who is this?"

"You don't recognize my voice? It's your grandfather."

"My grandfather? Edwin is that you? I don't think we've ever talked on the phone. Or ever."

"Yes, well, that's because your grandmamma didn't let me call you."

I love my grandmamma, and I've heard of the kind of person my grandfather is. So I call this bullshit.

"Edwin, I didn't have the best flight, and I'm really busy. What do you want?"

"No need to be hostile with me, Lizzie. I may be your only friend here."

"That's not true at all! I have many friends in London. I-in fact, I'll be going out with a friend tonight!" I quickly retort with a lie.

"I like your spirit, Lizzie. It reminds me of Evelyn."

"Edwin, save it."

"I'll see you on Monday?"

"Whatever."

"Looking forward to it, Lizzie."

"It's Eliza. Good night, Edwin."

Edwin Walker, my grandfather, is one person in my life I was taught to hate. He was kept at a distance from me. Or he kept his distance. I don't know. What I do know is that mom made sure I was aware of how much she hated him.

With nearly a hundred items around the house I need to log manually, I decide I better get on with the work.

My trusted laptop is gone, and thinking about it, my heart sinks. Dad couldn't afford to buy me a laptop at all. I accidently opened a letter from their bank. The house they live in, the house *I* live in will be repossessed if they don't pay by the end of the next month. Mom hasn't been working for a long time and dad cannot pay the bills all by himself, even though he works sixty hours a week. And on top of that, there's mom's breast cancer surgery. Ugh.

I pick up a piece of paper and a pen, and start walking around, observing my workload, going from room to room throughout the house. It feels overwhelming, grandmamma has a lot of stuff, most covered with dust from not being opened or touched in years.

After a thorough expedition around every nook and cranny in the house, I sit on the living room's floor, and start working. It's where most of the stuff is, or at least where the majority of the furniture items are. Without the list mom gave me I'm going by memory, and I'm hoping I won't miss a lot.

The house is enormous and old, it creaks eerily, and every now and again I'd stop and listen for the noises. It's unnerving, being here alone. After the afternoon I've had, I haven't really switched off, I'm still distraught.

I start with describing in my notebook each item I'm seeing, and then I stand up and mark it with one of the small white stickers I found in one of the kitchen drawers. Each room in this four bedroom house is full of things, some old, some new. The hallways, the bathrooms, the storage cabinets, the cloakroom, every nook and cranny. I have no idea if they are worth anything. My task is to note down every single item I see in the house. Hopefully they'll be pushed at auction and mom will get the money she so desperately needs.

But then, even if she gets better, I'd still be adopted.

"We are not your parents. Do you understand that?"

Understand? Do they understand that I've been walking on the streets every day since they told me, staring at the people, searching for someone I resemble? I'm hanging out with my birth relatives in my head, imagining the life I would have had if I hadn't been adopted.

I keep working until the early hours of the Saturday morning, meticulously recording details, every now and again my mind jumping to Sean.

At one o'clock in the morning, I'm not tired, if I was in Boston the time would have been nine in the evening.

I lean back on the sofa for a little rest when, I think, I hear movement upstairs. Someone is walking on the old creaking floorboards. Immediately my heart jumps out of my chest, it starts beating faster as the influx of adrenaline courses through my body. My fight or flight mode switches on and I stand up quickly. *Where am I going to go now?* The light is on in the living room, but it's dark in the hallway, and upstairs. I run to the wall, switch it off and wait by it for my eyes to adjust to the darkness. Once I know where I am I silently walk outside of the room and into the hallway. Whoever is upstairs is now standing on the landing and trying to adjust to the space, to figure out where I am. Without making a sound I tiptoe towards the kitchen, and to the back door leading to the garden when, the bell of the front door ringing and a few hard knocks instantly make me expel a rush of air in the form of a stunted scream.

"Eliza?" *Sean?* He's heard my voice, but the man upstairs did too. Conscious that I'm in the hallway, he rushes down the stairs, towards me.

"Sean, help me!" I shout and run to the kitchen, towards the back door. I try to open it but it's locked. And the key is not there. A flash back of grandmamma saying she keeps the key under the flowerpot in the corner, next to the door, comes to my mind, and frenziedly I start feeling the floor, searching for the damned flowerpot. But the man is faster. Running into the kitchen with a jagged breath, he tangles his thick fingers in my hair, and yanks me up. I squeal in pain. Both of my hands clutch his arm, grasping it as tightly as he's pulling on my hair. I claw at the skin of his arm, trying to pull him off, but he is strong.

"Don't fucking move!" He orders in his gruff voice as he switches the light on. His breath, coming from his unkempt disgusting beard, makes me gag. His pungent body odor makes my face distort. It's vile.

Sean is swearing outside as he tries to unsuccessfully knock down the door with his shoulder. Or whatever it is that he thuds on the door with.

"Why are you here? Take everything in this house, just let me go! What do you want??" Yanked up, I'm still half the height of the repulsive man in front of me.

"You," he says as he's speedily tying my hands with a zip tie in front of me.

"Who? Who wants me? Why? WHY?!"

The man looks forcefully in my eyes, as if trying to see something. I'm taken aback by his bloodcurdling stare, his nostrils flared.

"You know why."

"I don't! I don't! Tell me!"

"They will. Soon." He pulls out a gun and with the butt of it he breaks the lock on the back door. Then he tugs me by my upper arm, and drags me with him.

A sudden gunshot makes us both crouch; it must be Sean, and he's shot through the front door.

"Get your hands off her! Now! Do it!" He's charging inside like a raging bull.

Instantly the goon releases me and I don't wait, I break free and run to Sean as my kidnapper points his gun towards him. Sean pushes me aside and pulls the trigger again, this time wounding the thug, who shrieks in pain. Nevertheless, the thug aims his gun at Sean just as I jump in front of him, which makes him hesitate and curse loudly. Sean shoots again but this time misses, as the thug turns around, and runs into the garden, disappearing somewhere in the dark.

"Dammit, he'll get away!" Sean is furious and about to run after him but I hold him in my embrace, my arms locked behind his neck, my face forcefully pressing over his chest.

"Why did you do that? He could have killed you!"

My arms tighten stronger around him.

"Are you okay, Eliza? Did he do something to you?" He pinches my chin and lifts my head, anxiously looking at my eyes, and all over my face, searching of any sign of hurt.

"Y-you saved me again."

I'm gazing at him with teary eyes. I cannot contain the fear flooding my soul. It's coming out, and it's unsettling. His blue, hooded eyes offer me refuge.

"H-he tied me up," I lift my hands above his head and show them to him.

Instantly he finds a knife and cuts the zip tie digging into the skin around my wrists.

"Why is this happening to me?" I hear myself whisper.

He rakes his fingers through his hair in defeat.

"Someone wants you real bad. You're lucky I came back."

"Y-yeah. T-thank you. W-why did you come back?"

"I got something for you and I didn't want to wait until tomorrow to give it to you. I wanted to see you again."

"Sean, please don't leave me alone."

"I won't, I promise. We'll find someplace for you to crash. Come, many people would have heard the gunshots. The man that tried to kidnap you is wounded, and it shouldn't be hard tracking him down. I must go to see Darby again. I know he'll find him."

"Where am I going?"

He places his hand on my lower back protectively and leads me back via the hallway and out through the broken door. "I'll keep you safe, I promise."

"And this? The house is open, people could take everything." There's wooden shards spread all over from the bullet going through the door lock.

He pulls his cell out of his pocket and calls a number. While waiting for whoever it is to answer, he picks up a bag that's lying on the grass, and passes it to me.

"Here, I got something for you to wear until you sort yourself out. There is a cell phone in there, too. Call your folks, tell them you are okay."

"Darby, it's me. Someone tried kidnapping her again. - The address I gave you. - I broke the front door to get to her. - The house is riddled with bullets. - One person. - Send someone over to bolt it. She won't be staying there anymore," he cuts the line and looks at me pressing the buttons of my new cell. It's old, one of those flip phones that you use for calling, and maybe texting.

"Come on, we'll grab a cab from Kings Road."

"Where are we going?"

"To the police station."

Within minutes we pick up a black cab, and after giving the driver directions towards the other end of Kings Road, Sean switches off the buttons that connects our communication with the driver and turns to me. I wait for him to say something but he just observes me, my tattered skirt and my white t-shirt.

"Are you cold?"

"A little."

"There should be a sweatshirt somewhere in there," pointing to the bag he gave me.

I take the bag on my knees and unzip it.
There are a few short-sleeved tops, a few
denim skirts, pair of trousers, a few dresses
and one sweatshirt. Plus and a pair of
Converse sneakers, half a size bigger than
mine. First thing I do is put the sneakers on.
My flats are not very comfortable and half a
size won't make any difference.

"Whose are these?"

"Yours now."

CHAPTER 5

Darby Kent would have been a nice man if he didn't disturbingly stare at me and asked me to repeat my name at least ten times, as if he didn't believe me at all. Then he kept assuring me everything is okay, but I knew what a farce that was. I answered a ton of questions, and still doubt I helped. I know nothing. Why would anyone want to kidnap me is beyond my understanding. What they should do is find whoever is responsible for this, before it's too late.

In this dreadful and grey concrete police station, I've never wanted my mom and dad so much. I'm miles away from home, alone, and afraid. I wanted to call dad, to tell him what had happened to me, but then…. How could he help me? He couldn't. He wouldn't come here, we don't have that money. Money. That's what is important. As long as

I get to that meeting on Monday morning and have the money by the end of next week for mom, dad would be happy. He's at work, anyway. He wouldn't pick up his cell.

Sean O'Connell is the only person that reminds me of home. Of feeling safe. He's in the adjacent office, separated from me with a clear glass, sitting with the artist who is making an e-fit drawing of the man who wanted to kidnap me. He is talking to him, all the while looking at me through the glass. I glance in his direction a few times, I need that shot of security his eyes radiate. Each time our eyes meet, his lips would go in a straight line, and he would nod. As if he is telling me he is watching, not to worry.

But I do worry. So much.

I'm supposed to hate Sean, as he's a man. But I kind of like him. I'm grateful he saved me, twice.

"We're done in here," Sean is standing at the doorframe, as tall as the door itself. Under the sterile light, his eyes look like the skies have dawned a clear, blazing blue. Darby stands up and joins him by the door.

"Where are you taking her?" I barely hear Darby's voice.

"She's coming with me," Sean calmly replies, turning his back to me.

"Sean…- "

"Don't." He growls at Darby.

"Wh-where am I going?"

"You'll be staying with me tonight. Come on, let's not waste any more time. It's been a long day."

I look at Darby, but he just shrugs his shoulders. Sean has already put his jacket on.

"Shall we?"

I pick up the bag he gave me, and we leave the room through the glass door and head towards the stairs.

"Where are we going?"

"Hotel. You'll stay the night with me. In the morning I'll take you back to your house."

I'm going to sleep in his hotel room.

The mere thought frightens me as much as the actual kidnapping does.

Twenty minutes later we arrive in front of Royal Garden Hotel, a concrete building from the sixties, situated conveniently on Kensington High Street, adjacent to the Kensington Palace and its gardens. The valet outside runs to the cab to open the door, and welcomes us with a French accent. With a reserved smile on his face, Sean just tucks a banknote into his jacket.

"Thank you, I'll take it from here."

"Of course," the valet takes a few steps backwards, and discreetly slots into his place by the door.

We go up the staircase and enter the lobby of the hotel when the Hotel Manager, that's what it says on his nametag, approaches us with open hands.

"Mr. O'Connell!"

"Fernando, how are you?" Sean shakes his hand.

"Very well, thank you! We have your room ready, Mr. O'Connell. Your bag arrived from the airport this evening. It's in there."

"Excellent, thank you."

The Hotel Manager looks at me while I stand awkwardly, out of place, with the bag in my hand. "And who is this lovely lady?"

"Miss Eliza Cruz. She'll be staying with me tonight," Sean says matter of fact. "Fernando, do you think we can get something to eat at this time of the night?"

"Of course, Mr. O'Connell. Leave it to me," he nods and steps aside.

We proceed to walk up the stairs, along the landing, and stop in front of the last room at the end of the long hallway.

Sean unlocks the door, opens it and waits for me to enter. Hesitantly I walk inside, my eyes alarmingly searching for a second bed, but there's none.

He takes off his brown leather jacket, and throws it on the chair. His t-shirt, stretched over his chest and stomach, is showing off his defining muscular lines running down to his groin. Then he rakes his hair with his fingers as he sits on the bed.

I must look like a petrified doe on a highway. My heart will jump out of my chest any second now. Only my breathing is slow, measured.

"What's the matter, beautiful?"

"Nothing."

"Something's on your mind."

"Um, what he said," I divert my thoughts by proxy. I must or else I'll go insane.

"He?"

"The man in grandmamma's house. He said 'they' wanted me, and when I asked who and why, he looked at me as if I should know."

"Did you tell Darby?"

"Yes."

I drop my bag on the floor and bravely inhale. If I'm going to do this, I'm going to suck it up. I walk over and sit down on the bed, next to Sean.

"Look, I'm really sorry, Sean. I'm sorry I don't have anyone to take me in. I promise you first thing tomorrow I'm going back to grandmamma's house. I'll fix the door. I - ,"

"It's okay, don't worry."

"I don't want to be a burden. You don't need to be looking after me. I must have messed up your plans, too. I'm really sorry."

"You haven't. My plans don't start until tomorrow so don't apologize."

"There has to be some kind of misunderstanding. I know it's not me they are looking for."

"How do you know?"

I shrug with my shoulders. "They must have the wrong girl. I've been to England only once before. And recently I was told I was adopted, so I know this cannot have anything to do with me. It turns out grandmamma is not my real grandmamma anymore, and that's the end of the story."

"End of the story?!"

I nod.

"Do you think the story ends there? So what if you are adopted? You're not the first or the last person on the earth to be adopted."

Instantly I hear a growl inside me, and then out loud, aimed at him.

"Mind your own fucking business, Sean."

"You don't have the right to feel bad about being adopted, Eliza. That was not your decision to make."

"It's my decision … It's my decision to know… ugh!" I curl my fingers into a fist and swing, nearly punching him right under his chin when he grabs my clenched hand and twists it backwards, making my whole body yield under his strength. I'm almost lying on the bed, bent under Sean's firm grasp of my fist, when I realize his body is close to my mouth and I lunge for his pecs with my teeth. He pulls back, still not letting go of me.

"Fuck, Eliza, what are you doing? I don't want to hurt you."

"Let-me-go!" I huff through my teeth as I'm twisting in pain.

He pushes me off, releasing my arm and I fall on the bed. I lay down, massaging my wrist with my other hand, and watching him from below.

"Well you did hurt me."

"Let me see what I've done," he reaches with his hands to check my wrist when I swiftly lift my leg and head for a kick in his head. *I bet he is not expecting this!*

With a speed of light he grabs my foot and lies down, and with his legs he locks my body in an impossible position to free myself.

Okay. He wins. Obviously.

"What the fuck is wrong with you?" He barks.

"What the fuck is wrong with *you*?! Why are you showing off?"

"Showing off? Are you mad?"

I struggle against his weight, try to set myself free but I'm unsuccessful.

"Let me go!"

He pushes me over to fall on my stomach and straddles my thighs. My arms are twisted behind my back, as if he's making an arrest. Fucker, I can't move.

"You have to stop fighting me or I'll handcuff you to the bed if I have to. Do you understand?"

This is it. The moment mom was telling me about. In panic I turn behind me, searching for his eyes. But what I see is not threat, or danger, but inexplicable spark that stirs me. I don't know how to translate it. Shiver runs through me the moment he glances at my lips. And his hips move forward. Or I may have imagined it. I just know that I lose it right then. I snarl, bucking up and down to try to get him off of me, but he's heavy.

"Whoa, easy now," I twist and turn and he manages to flip me over, now sitting on top of me, straddling my hips, and holding my arms pinned on the bed above my head. I don't like this position at all. He's perched above me, his eyes roaming all over my face.

"Dammit, Eliza …,"

"Let-me-go!"

He shakes his head. "It's impossible when you are wild like this."

I stop struggling, and glare at his intense eyes, in hope to deflect him but it's the opposite. He's coming closer.

"Don't you dare! Sean –,"

He leans down, forcefully parting my lips with his, and thrusting his tongue inside my mouth, deep, kissing me so violently our teeth clash. I gasp, and pull back, but there's nowhere further to go from the mattress behind me. He kisses me again, possessively his tongue weaves inside my mouth, setting my mind, body and soul on fire. His body's pressing flat against mine as his tongue's thrusting is melting me down. The moment it ends, I know I've surrendered.

He pulls back, panting, his eyes burning alight.

"Goddamn Eliza, stop doing that!"

"Doing what?" I'm breathless from his kiss.

"Provoking me!"

"But… I didn't."

He releases my hands, and gets off of me. "Anyway, you are fighting ghosts. Give it up."

He brings me back into reality too soon.

"That's not the way to live your life. It's not your battle to fight. It's done now. It's over. Someone else fought it for you. In your honor. Appreciate them, dammit!" He slams the door of the bathroom. I hear him turning the shower on, and the sound of the water infusing the cubicle.

"Mind your own fucking business, Sean!" I yell, making sure he hears me, but I tremble inside. His kiss moved a few tectonic plates inside my body.

That day I recited Milli's letter to the men in the room, with everyone sitting down at a round table, staring at me. The Luminary, as they called him, stood up. He was the leader of this nightmarish ring. He must have been in his forties; tall, grey hair, clean shave. Perfectly fitted suit. Just like the others. Their suits were immaculate. And all the same, navy blue with shiny gold cufflinks.

"The road to heaven is paved with pleasure, for all of us," his voice was ominous. "We are ready to take you, Milli."

"I don't want to be here. Please, let me go," I ended on a whisper. There were tears rolling down my cheeks as the men were staring, their lips crooked, some were groping their crotch, and one made a fist and bit it with his mouth agape.

"How can I? Look at them, they are impatient."

I raised my chin in defiance, my tears proudly shining on my skin. They will never take me. I'd rather die.

"Eventually, your spirit will break, and you will learn to love us, as ugly as we come."

"Never."

"Milli, don't forget how much we'd do for you. All of us, devoted and faithful to you, and you only. And you should be, too."

His eyes kept going up and down my body, taking away my innocence. The clothes I had on were taken from me, they left me barely with anything to change in. A skimpy floor length robe in a see-through netting and nothing underneath. It was meaningless wearing it but since I was not allowed to dress myself, the men doing it decided for me.

"We'll arrange for you to have a husband while you look after your daughter, but not for long. Two years only, those are the years that you'll have your rest, of course. Then you'll come right back in our loving arms."

There was a moments' silence before my head caught on with what he said.

"M-my daughter?"

"Yes. How do you think we know who you are? We breed your kind every twenty years. Actually, only the Luminary does the breeding, and then, it's open season for everyone."

My eyes opened wide, I gasped as I covered my mouth with my hand.

"Y-ou are m-my f-father?"

"No. But I'll be the father of the next Milli in line. I am your breeder for the next twenty years. Your father was the Luminary before me. When we took you, he was dismissed. We are not animals in here Milli, we love your kind, and look after you."

My chest hurt as I was taking information too vile to absorb. Everything hurt. I tried logically to sort my spine-chilling thoughts, but there wasn't any sense in it. And then, it dawned on me as fast as a bolt of lightning. Dread and horror lashed my body. I rejected my tears, and right at that moment, I refused to accept my fate. Because that would mean I'd imagine my life in here. And I couldn't.

"Wh-what if I have a son?"

"They'd be given up for adoption. But so far there never were any boys. Your bloodline is strong. You've given us only girls. This makes us believe in Milli and her wish even more so. And as soon as you are with child, you'll get your keeper, your make believe husband, for two years."

"And after?"

"After you'll come back here, on your own. Once with a child, we know you won't run away."

"How do you know that?"

"You'll become addicted. You'll be coming for more every day, twice, or three times. And sometimes, you'd stay the night."

In hell I might.

"D-drugs?"

"Love."

I frown in disgust.

"We love you, Milli, all of us do. We're here to serve You. You'll be happy to hear that this year we were inundated with applications. The ten men in front of you may become fifty soon. So enjoy the intimacy of tonight. You may not get it in the future."

CHAPTER 6

Half an hour later Sean comes out of the bathroom. His face is clean-shaven, smooth, his hair is combed back, he's wearing a long towel around his hips. There are stray water droplets running down his pectorals, glistening under the light. I'm on the bed, playing with the cell he gave me, and covertly looking at him.

"Eliza," he rakes his fingers through his wet hair, messing it up. "I... um, I was out of order. I'm sorry."

"I'm sorry, too," I reply quietly, looking at my cell.

He frowns. "What are *you* sorry for?"

"Well, you know. For being a spoilt brat. Sometimes I can't control myself," I press a few buttons on my cell, and listen to the various tones they make. "And sometimes I'm just socially inept."

"Where have you been all your life? Locked up in a tower?"

"Home schooled."

"Adopted and home-schooled," he shakes his head while heading towards the wardrobe. "How on earth did your parents let you come here all by yourself?"

I see him opening the wardrobe door and upon finding his bag, he picks up a few clothes and stands behind it. I shrug with my shoulders. *Money.* I want to tell him but choose not to. Even *I* have stupid pride.

"Well?" He asks from behind it.

"Um, my mom is at the hospital. Dad is with her all the time. I don't think they really are thinking of me right now."

"I'm sure they do."

"Whatever."

"Me? I'm heading to France tomorrow."

I didn't ask.

"Oh… Where to?"

"A little village close to Saint Tropes. It's called Lacoste."

Having finished dressing up, he carefully closes the wardrobe doors, and wearing black slacks and black t-shirt, he strides towards me. His eyes seem hooded, intense. I awkwardly crook my lips but he doesn't reciprocate. At this proximity, I must keep talking.

"Wh-What did you apologize for?"

"For many things. But mainly for not being able to control myself around you," standing too close, his eyes are focused on my lips. Slowly, he reaches out and takes my jaw in his hand. "Dammit, Eliza, has anyone told you how beautiful you are?"

"You did. At least ten times today."

As if he didn't just apologize for the crime he's about to commit, he leans in and places a strong, passionate kiss on my lips while holding my jaw firmly in his hand. He pulls back for a second and looks at my eyes, and all over my face, then tangles his fingers deep in my hair and pulls me to him again. He parts my lips and inserts his tongue in a rush, searching to weave it with mine, passing his craving on to me. All of a sudden I'm pinned down on the bed, his body pressing mine fully. His hands hold my wrists and it's too late when I realize he's nested between my legs, changing the pressure to his sporadic grinding. My legs are gradually turning to jelly and amid the pleasure, I'm confused. Sex has never been on the plate for me but now I wonder if this is what people talk about. I copy his movements, grind into him too, and a strange unforeseen moan comes out of my lips.

He buries his head in my neck, and his hot, wet lips are now running down my neckline. My wrists are in his hands held above my head. I'm losing my sight with … something. Fuck knows what, but what he does to me is driving me crazy. My eyes are closed, I dare not look at him, only I try to move, to pull my hands down but I can't. He's holding me firmly in place, while his tongue is running havoc under my skin.

"Sean, I… I mustn't," I have to voice my objection, even in theory. This is too good to pass in practice. This is heaven. Why didn't mom tell me? What is wrong here? The only thing I'm aware of is the road to something… the build-up inside my head.

"No, *I* mustn't, but I can't resist you. You are mouth-watering," he mumbles over my skin as he releases my hands.

Uninhibited, I'm flying high under the crusade of his wandering hand when I feel it, suddenly, skin on skin, his palm over my left breast. Startled I stop, and open my eyes but there's not much I can do. I'm simply someone observing from aside, watching him pulling the cups of my bra down and pushing my breasts up, and out of it. My breasts aren't small, a D cup that now looks bigger, are perked up, my nipples hardened and he's approaching them at alarming speed. The moment his tongue touches my nipple, I surrender my soul to the devil. Warm wet tongue is sucking on me, my whole body shaking from the deliverance. I moan, and with eyes half closed I see him holding my hardened nipple between his teeth. Suddenly a throbbing pain shoots through my body. I whine as he tugs on my nipple, my body curving, following him.

"Sean…"

He releases my nipple and stops, poignantly waiting on me to finish my sentence. I wasn't going to say anything. If I could I'd probably say "More, please," but I shouldn't voice my opinion. I close my eyes and inhale, arching my body, aching for contact.

Mercifully he continues, his lips reaching the mound of my right breast and ever so gently he latches on it. The moment I feel his teeth again, an electric shock zaps inside my body. I know what I want. But I can't say it. I'm not allowed.

"Little wanton girl, what are you doing to me?"

I hear him say as he goes south, past my belly, and lifts my skirt up. I feel his hands on my inner thighs, slowly spreading my legs. As he positions himself down there, I have this urge to push him off, to close my legs. And I try, I do, a few times but as much I fight against his strength, my body wants to submit to his desires. My excuse – I still have my panties on. And he can't do much if my panties are on. I think. *Shush, my overactive mind.*

I hear him loudly inhaling my scent, and feel something gently gliding over my panties, his fingers maybe. I moan, and scrunch the bed sheet for leverage. My …My gem is getting tarnished. *But I have my panties on.* And the moment I feel something harder down there, ripples of desire burst through me. Something is undeniably coming closer, and it's going to make me explode. *But I got my panties on!?*

I moan loud, and my hips move impulsively as his fingers pull my panties aside, and something wet thrusts gently inside me.

"S-sean…," I moan. I'm getting close to an eruption, my hips are strangely dancing in the air, and I can't take it anymore. I glance down at him; I'm being devoured but something is wrong, everything slows down. There's not enough force. I moan, softly at first, then louder, I'm not making sense at all. He's turned me into this lewd creature that I can't control.

Suddenly he stands up, takes my hand and pulls me up on the bed in front of him. I'm on my knees, turned with my back to him, legs apart. He wraps one hand around my waist and pulls me flat against his solid body, and the other, the other… Oh my

God! I moan but it's more of a scream this time. His fingers are inside me, and with each trust I feel the eruption closer.

"Ride it, baby, ride it," he orders into my ear.

His words make me lose myself in the flurry of butterflies amassed by the dance of my hips. I cry at the intensity of the moment, completely lost in the abundance of vibrations going into different parts of my body. My incoherent moans are a true witness to what my body is going through. My legs buck, but he holds my body tight, and allows me to feel the recurring ripples coming from his fingers.

I lean my body on his, and realize that I have a few tears rolling down my cheek. I don't want to move, I don't want him to see my tears. I wasn't crying. I was flying. I wipe my tears as he comes in front of me and embraces me.

"Eliza, are you okay?"

I nod. I just hope Sean is nothing like the men mom described

We lay on the bed for the next ten minutes in silence, his arms wrapped around me. The sudden knock on the door startles us.

Sean jumps out of bed and grabs his gun. I could swear by looking at him there seems to be another gun in his slacks. Quietly he approaches the door and looks through the peephole while I cover myself with the bed sheet.

"It's room service," he mouths and opens the door slightly. He sends the waiter off and wheels a small cart with food under two silver domed plates.

He's not wasting any time, he's removing the sliver domes, and checking the food on the plates - steak and potatoes.

"It smells delicious."

Now that the heavy, lingering desire I had pressing between my thighs is gone, the smell fills my nostrils and reaches my empty stomach, another craving is ensuing – food. I don't remember when was the last time I ate. I'm famished. He proceeds to place the plates and the cutlery on the table. Then he picks up the bottle of red wine and checks the small print.

"Perfect."

He takes the wine glasses from the trolley, and pours wine in his glass. Then he salutes me, and drinks it fully. He refills his glass, and looks at me.

"Drink?"

I clear my throat. "Yes, I'll be drinking."

"Shall we eat?"

I nod, and straighten the crumpled clothes on my body while getting off of the bed. My legs are still wobbly and glancing at his large protrusion in his slacks, I have a feeling that he's going to ask me to reciprocate the favor.

But he doesn't. He must be really hungry. He sits at the table and waits on me to do the same. Then he picks up his fork and knife, and probably hope I'll mirror his action. I don't and so he looks at me as he cuts into his steak, and takes a morsel of food on his fork, biting into it possessively, chewing with his mouth closed.

The second piece of steak is speared on his fork, and he offers it to me. *Is he feeding me now?* I've read too many books on this subject. If a man feeds a woman he is enamored with her. *Fuck, Eliza, be cool!* But it's true! I swallow before opening my mouth, not sure what to expect.

"Eat," he orders.

I'm holding my mouth open with the meat inside, and after a second I realize he's waiting on me to tug it off of his fork. In an instant I take it, and start chewing, hoping and praying he doesn't see how stupid I look.

"Good?"

"Mmm, yes."

We don't say a word during our meal. Only, as we are eating, he's silently observing me, which really, takes me back to hell.

I had to remember every word in that letter by heart. To know thyself, they said. To know what I am. And who I am.

I've never heard of Marquis de Sade before. But having been forced to read about him in this small confined space, on my knees with my bottom out of that wretched hole, I now know who Milli was. These books say her sexual gratification depended on suffering physical pain and humiliation. She was gratified by pain imposed by others. And they are priming me for the same, for the big cull, as they say.

But the fighter in me doesn't miss a beat.

She listens to them. How they communicate, what they say and what they don't say. She absorbs everything.

For example, I know the Luminary in this generation is special. He'll give blue blood to the next creation of Millis.

Unfortunately, he is the only one with the key to unlock my space, and to make me do things. To torture me in bewildering ways. He has done it twice within the two months I'm here. I don't know how long it will take him to break me. But I do know that no matter what they do to me, I won't give in.

I am unbreakable. I can take it.

If I focus on escaping this hell hole alive, it would matter. To me. To the next generations.

CHAPTER 7

It must be late in the morning; the sun is bright, and high in the sky. I raise my head, looking for Sean, and see him sitting at the table reading a newspaper with a cup of coffee in front of him. His hair is wet, and combed back, giving him a sleek look. This morning he looks different. His clothes are different too. He's wearing suit pants, white shirt with the sleeves folded three quarters up, tight fitting vest and a black tie. A navy blue jacket is hanging on the corner of the bed. This morning he looks like an adult. An irresistible adult.

Last night we slept together, but nothing else happened. He didn't try to kiss me again, he just held me tight all night as if I was the only woman left in this world. I had to take my clothes off, bar my panties, because it was too hot in the bed. Still, even with his hard protrusion, he didn't try anything. I wrapped myself in the sheet, and then, in his arms, all night. Mom would not approve, that's for sure.

Realizing I'm practically naked, I make sure the sheet is properly wrapped around my body before I get up, pick up the bag he gave me last night and start tiptoeing towards the bathroom. Hopefully he's engrossed in the newspaper he's reading, and he can't see me.

"You're up," Sean's voice startles me. I stop, and look at him, if the bed sheet were wrapped any tighter around my body I'd be a walking mummy. Luckily he's not really paying any attention to my theatricals, and so I use the moment to hurry towards the bathroom.

"Yes. Give me a minute to dress up," before closing the door I see him in the reflection of the mirror inside, checking me out. I can't help but smile as I lock the door.

I remove the sheet and take my panties off, and turn on the shower. The hot torrent falling down my body feels most needed. Reflecting back on last night as I'm lathering my skin, my focus is on washing off my sins. Was what we did last night a sin? Mom had always said I should never have sex with a man, or at least wait until I get married, and I haven't, honest to God. But I did something else. Sean touched me. Yet, he didn't ask me to reciprocate.

After the dinner last night, we didn't say much. I know I felt guilty as hell, but Sean also had something on his mind. Guilt? I doubt it. That was reserved for me only, courtesy of my selfish mother.

I finish my shower and I'm on to phase two of my dressing up - rummaging through the clothes in the bag. I wonder whose clothes are these. Most of them are a size bigger, apart from the pleated above-the-knee black skirt, which fits me perfectly. The plain white t-shirt is also on the large side, but with my breasts filling it up aptly, it fits.

And, of course, there are no panties. Anyway I wasn't really hoping to borrow panties from someone I don't know. Dammit. I'll go without up to the first shop on the road that sells them.

"Breakfast is here," Sean knocks on the door.

"I'll be right out."

I dry my hair as best as I can, and brush it quickly. It falls down to below my shoulders, and as it's still wet, droplets form and roll down, soaking into my t-shirt.

I take a deep breath and unlock the door.

"Good morning."

Upon seeing me Sean stands up like a gentleman and pulls up a chair for me. When he's certain I'm sitting comfortably, he walks back to his side and sits down. Today, he's a different person. Almost unrecognizable. Miles away from the rugged look he had last night. Not that he wasn't a gentleman last night, it's just, the clothes make him look rather suave.

"Eliza, look at you. You look gorgeous."

"Thank you. You look… Different."

"Good different?"

I nod, embarrassed, and gently pull the saucer holding the hot coffee cup. There are croissants on the table, and jam. The aroma is so appealing, it makes me think I haven't eaten in days. As I take the coffee to my mouth I remember how sore my lips are. And then, a flash back from last night comes to my mind and my lips crook shyly.

"Did you have a good night, Eliza?"

"Yes. I-I liked last night."

"I meant, did you sleep well?"

"Oh. I, um, yes. Thank you." Mortified, I train my eyes on the coffee cup.

"So did I. On both counts, of course," there is a ghost of a smile in his voice.

"But y-you didn't - ,"

He leans on the table, towards me, clearly amused. I lift my eyes and meet his steady gaze.

"I didn't what, Eliza?"

"You, um…"

"Do you feel guilty that I didn't come?"

I stare at him, speechless. *Where's my voice gone?*

"If you wanted to do something about it you should have." He pauses. "Do you want to do something about it now?"

His eyes penetrate down to the very core he shook last night.

I open my mouth, hoping to say something coherent when his laughter interrupts me.

"I'm only teasing, Eliza. Please forgive me. I don't have to come to have a good time, beautiful. Trust me."

Relieved, I smile too. I'm not sure what I would have said anyway.

"But I do want to spend more time with you today." He gently strokes my hand with the back of his.

"W-what about France?"

"I postponed France."

"You shouldn't have. I need to go to grandmamma's house to finish the work today. Monday is my deadline. I'm busy, Sean."

"Have you ever been a tourist in London, Eliza?"

"No."

"I'd like to be your tour guide today, if you don't mind."

"I don't need a tour guide, Sean."

"You do if you want to know about London's harrowing history."

"What makes you think I want to know about London's harrowing past?"

"Isn't it always more fun to learn about the gruesome and grotesque history than the obvious one? Don't you want to find out about the real London, since you are already here?"

"I suppose."

"Trust me, you'll love it."

I'm busy. I have things to do. But his eyes, his whole presence makes me want to follow him to the end of the world.

"Let me make a few calls, and we'll head out in, say, ten minutes?"

"Sure." I take a croissant and stand up. "I'll have more coffee downstairs. You can finish your work in here."

"Take your cell phone with you. And don't go anywhere, stay in the hotel until I come downstairs."

I nod, leaving the room, and head down towards the reception.

The staircase is carpeted with a bright orange pattern which I'm certain causes me nausea. Still, I'm grateful. Sean took me in for the night, and I will not forget that.

Downstairs, I stop in the middle of the large hall, stunned at the sight. I wish I had my cell phone to take a picture of this amazing view. I tilt my head back, and spin slowly, hoping to absorb the space. It looks majestic.

After a moment of feeling lightheaded I look down again, and see Sean, standing on the staircase, regarding me calmly with his jacket over his shoulder.

I smile. He does too, and saunters down the stairs, towards me. The man yesterday was rugged, racing cars, chasing culprits, shooting at them. And this one today is sophisticated in an unnerving way.

"Shall we?"

I nod. He places his hand on my lower back, his fingers curling around my waist, and guides me with him outside. "The taxi is waiting for us."

After thirty minutes ride, which take us right in the middle of London, the taxi drops us on Tower Bridge.

"The Tower of London?" I ask, surprised.

"Don't tell me you've been here."

"I haven't. I've heard of it though. You?"

"Last time I visited the Tower of London was the day I turned twenty two. That was five years ago."

"You don't mind seeing it again?"

"It's the oldest place to visit in London. Of course I don't mind."

"Really?"

"You see the white tower protruding from inside the walls?" He points to a white stone building within the enclosure.

"Mhm."

"It was built in 1066 by William the Conqueror, the first Norman King of England, to awe, subdue and terrify Londoners and to deter foreign invaders. It's an iconic symbol of London and Britain."

"Also, and fuck me if I know how I got this information inside my head, the Tower has the oldest timeline on Facebook. They have virtually 1000 years of monumental dates to the Tower of London's timeline."

"That's interesting, I guess," I shrug with my shoulders. "I don't have a Facebook account so I wouldn't know."

"No? That's a first."

"Well, I was home sch-,"

"Home schooled, I know. Still, in this day and age that would be a great way to connect with your peers and discuss work, stuff... I don't know. Especially for home schooled kids."

"Yeah, I didn't have that. I was given internet carte blanche only a few years ago, but still I wouldn't search for sites or words that were off the limit. And at that time I hadn't seen what Facebook, Twitter, Snapchat, Instagram and the rest were like."

"What sites were off limits for you?"

"I don't know. I forgot them. I suppose all the adult sites and such. The first thing I checked when I was allowed was the social media. It wasn't that much fun anyway."

"It's not, I agree."

"So you're not on Facebook?"

"No."

"But you just said you know about the Tower of London being on Facebook."

"Yeah, I also said I don't know how I know."

"Twitter?"

"No."

"Instagram?"

Sean steps up in front of me, and I realize he's outside the ticket box office.

"Two tickets for the Tower of London, please," he says to the woman inside the booth. Then he looks at me and whispers, "What pictures am I going to post on Instagram? Of murderers? Blood?"

"Is that what you do?" I whisper too.

"What?"

"Kill people?"

He picks up the tickets and looks at me.

"Don't you remember seeing me yesterday shooting at someone?"

"Yes, but you didn't kill him."

"That's because I wanted him alive."

"Really?"

114

"Yes, otherwise he'd be dead."

"How many have you killed?"

"A few."

"A few?" My eyes open wide. He's a murderer? He's a murderer. Lawful murderer. Still, those are murderers too.

"Enough questions for now, let's get inside." He passes the tickets to the man at the entrance, and again, places his hand on my lower back protectively, allowing me to walk in front of him.

Inside the walls surrounding the Tower, is fascinating. It's Saturday and it's packed but the noise coming from the costumed live activity is loud enough for us to hear their brawl. The actors are involving everyone, summoning the audience to help the heroic guards defend the Tower against its medieval attackers. On the edge of the stage there are men dressed in red, but funny, the material reminding me of English folklore.

"Who are they?" I point towards them.

"Those are the Yeoman Warders, they are known as 'Beefeaters' nicknamed from their position in the Royal Bodyguard, which permitted them to eat as much beef as they wanted from the King's table. They've formed the Royal Bodyguard since at least five hundred years ago."

"You know quite a lot of history, Sean. Was that your major?"

"If I find something fascinating I tend to study it thoroughly. But right now, I'm hoping my knowledge of history will impress you. How's that working out by the way?"

"I am impressed," I shyly smile.

We reach the White Tower and walk up to the top of the stairs that lead inside it. But as we enter he takes me by my hand and we make way down a different staircase, and into a basement, where horrendous contraptions of torture are placed, some making my stomach churn.

"The British seemed to have the stomach for torture."

"You'd be surprised what the torture dungeons are like around Europe. It would make the hairs on the back of your neck stand out. This basement was the actual place where they tortured and interrogated prisoners such as Guy Fawkes."

"Was that the guy who wanted to blow up the Houses of Parliament in London, but failed?"

He stops and looks at me in surprise.

"What? I only know that because my dad and I visited London on November the 5th. That's when people make an effigy of Guy Fawkes and burn him on the night."

"Yes, the English are not taking it easy with traitors."

"What's that over there?" I point to an iron chair with nails protruding from every surface.

"That's the chair of torture. It's more like an intimidating torture device – the chair is layered with thousands of spikes on every surface with tight straps to restrain its victim. Over here, you see the large saw? That was used for saw torture. The victim is hung upside down, so that the blood will rush to their heads and keep them conscious during the long torture. The torturer would then saw through the victim's body until they were completely sawed in half. Most were cut up only to their abdomen to prolong their agony."

"Ugh. I feel queasy by just hearing that."

"And this one? It's called The Rack. A torture device with a roller at both ends. The victim's ankles are fastened to one roller and the wrists are chained to the other. As the interrogation progresses, a handle and ratchet mechanism attached to the top roller are used to gradually increase the tension on the chains, inducing excruciating pain. By means of pulleys and levers this roller could be rotated on its own axis, thus straining the ropes until the sufferer's joints were dislocated and eventually separated. Additionally, if muscles are stretched excessively, they lose their ability to contract, rendering them ineffective. One gruesome aspect of being stretched too far on the rack is the loud popping noises made by snapping cartilage, ligaments or bones."

"Um, I don't think I want to know anymore,"

I speed up my pace, but there are people around us and it's difficult to actually leave quickly. Also, the ones standing next to us are now looking at Sean and waiting on him to continue with his tour, so to say.

"Excuse me, do you know what sort of torture instrument is this one? It looks familiar, and I know it's something to do with women rather than men but I can't put my finger to it." An old woman with German accent asks him.

Sean looks at the iron made strange fork while I wonder if I want to know too or not. Before I decide, he starts speaking.

"You're right. This is a breast ripper."

All women in this stuffy stone cold basement groan. I do, too. My stomach really will not manage at this tempo.

"It's known as simply the spider, and it was mainly used on women who were accused of adultery. It's designed to rip the breasts from a woman and as it's made from iron, it was usually heated before use. The tool was used mainly in Bavaria, a state in Germany but it went all over Europe, as we can clearly see it."

"Yes, now I remember!" The old woman exclaims. "I've seen this somewhere in Deutschland."

Sean smiles politely and regarding me walking away, he hurries after me. He manages to reach me as I'm walking up the staircase.

"Eliza, wait!"

"It's fine Sean, you go ahead and stay, I will wait for you upstairs."

"No, no. I've been here already, too many times. I know all this. I thought you'd be enjoying the tour, that's all."

"That's gut wrenching, why would I be enjoying it?"

"You got to take it at face value. Come on, grow some balls."

"I have balls!" I narrow my eyes at him and take a step closer, my hands curling into fists.

"Okay. I believe you. Stop, okay. I don't want to fight you in front of all these people. I know what we can do instead."

"What?" Anything sounds better than the basement we were in right now.

"There is a tour bus that goes from here down to central London. It's an open top bus - we won't be going out but driving past most buildings. What do you say?"

"That sounds better than being in here."

"Great."

"Let's go," I take his hand, feeling a bit unnerved as I haven't taken a man's hand before, and drag him among the people. We manage to leave the surrounding walls of the Tower, and we end up in the middle of a crowded square.

"Right. Now where?"

"Over there," he points to another ticket booth. "I'll get tickets."

"Here, I have money," I reach into my skirt pocket, where my cell and the fifty pounds note from Anna is, and immediately he stops me by placing his hand firmly over mine.

"Eliza, please. It's out of the question."

"But-,"

"It's not my money I'm spending anyway, so please, don't feel like you have to pay for anything."

"What do you mean?"

"The FBI pays for my trip. France, England, wherever I go, they pay me."

"D-does that mean that you are working right now?"

"I'm always working," he states while looking for something in front, the tour bus perhaps.

"A secret mission?" I say quietly and stop walking, which makes him stop, too.

He regards me for a moment before pulling me close, and running his thumb over my lips. Then he leans in and plants a kiss over my mouth so soft, it makes me question my whole existence. I came here to help mom and dad, and so far I've done everything but. He inhales the air from my lungs and just as quickly, he pulls back, his lips shiny with remnants of our kiss.

He smiles broadly as if he knew what he'd done to me. He takes my hand and starts walking, eyes locked together. "Come on, let's not miss the bus."

We reach the bus stop just in time to see the traditional red double-decker bus signed "The Original Tour" pulling in. The size of the bus is intimidating, and it makes Sean pull me to him yet again, my back flat against his front, and hold me there until it stops moving. The moment it grinds to a halt and the doors open, the bulk of the tourists flood out onto the street, with very little distance between them. Their direction - The Tower of London.

The two of us, together with ten people or so waiting to get in the bus get the green light from the driver, and we all walk inside, and straight up on the second deck.

"Where shall we sit?" I ask.

"Back. Always the back."

We take the two seats of the last row in the open top bus. The tour is rather unusual, the driver is the one talking into a microphone and we could either listen to him on the speakers or use the small headset in front of us to listen to him talk. There's not an actual tour guide.

I get in the double seat first, and Sean follows me. He turns his back to the aisle, wrapping his arm around my shoulder, and with the other he points towards the river.

"That's the river Thames."

"Really? I didn't know that," I mock.

"You wanted the boring London, so don't complain."

I look towards the buildings in front of me; there is a mixture of old and new, and together with the people below them, I realize that I actually like to sit up here, observing the town.

"I'm not complaining. In fact, I feel safe in here."

He touches my chin gently and pulls my head towards him, "You're always safe when I'm around."

I smile dejectedly, remembering what my life came to be the moment I stepped off the plane. Would I change something if I knew what awaited me? He pulls me to his lips, as if reminding me, and plants a soft kiss over mine. For whatever happened, maybe it's worth it.

"On your left hand side you'll see the oldest church in the city, "All Hallows" founded in 675 A.D. The undercroft has Roman pavement dating from the 2nd century A.D."

The driver talks into the speakers and we both look on our left, where the couple in front of us point towards.

"Did you know The Queen needs permission to enter the City of London? She may be the head of state for the United Kingdom as well as countries such as Canada and Australia, but Queen Elizabeth II is not allowed to enter the City of London without permission from the Lord Mayor. The royal website states: "The citizens of London, through the Corporation of the City, still retain their ancient privilege of being able to bar the Sovereign from entering their streets." Although if she ever did decide she fancied a jaunt to Liverpool Street, we're sure the Queen would be more than welcome."

I smile. Of course she won't be asking for permission. She's the Queen for God's sake.

"Any Americans on board?"

For a split of a second I thought about responding but I'm quickly discouraged by a group of middle aged women excitedly screaming. Yes, we all know, you are Americans. I roll my eyes. Sean smirks at my annoyance.

"I bet you didn't know that the British eat twice as many baked beans per head than the Americans!"

The women laugh loudly, and make some remark about flatulent Englishmen.

"On your left hand side you'll see in the distance a tall column, which is a monument built to commemorate the Great Fire of London that happened in 1666 and to celebrate the rebuilding of the City. It's erected near the place where the fire began, which was in Pudding Lane.

Sir Christopher Wren, Surveyor General to King Charles II and the architect of St. Paul's Cathedral, and his friend and colleague, Dr Robert Hooke, provided a design for a colossal column in the antique tradition, with a drum and a copper urn at the top from which flames emerge, symbolizing the Great Fire. The Monument, as it came to be called, is 61 metres high, the exact distance between it and the site in Pudding Lane where the fire began."

The driver continues with the talk, which I find rather fascinating, while maneuvering the double decker bus through the narrow streets of London.

"Although the Great Fire of London destroyed much of the city, only six people were killed. In all honesty, the fire did incinerate the plague, that preceded it for a year, when 100 000 Londoners died."

Sean's hand on my knee draws my attention away from the captivating history of London, and all of a sudden, the sound of the driver fades in the distance. He put it there in such soft way that I can't ignore it. I'm sure there's nothing to it, only my stupid mind making it bigger than it actually is. I look into the building everyone is now staring at when, I feel him softly stroking my skin. I clear my throat nervously as I look around, I'm shielded by his body in a way that no one can see me. While everyone gazes at the tall building that looks like a large shard, slowly, and clandestinely, his hand slides under my skirt.

I bite my lip, my heart beat speeds up and my legs close instinctively. His fingers are burning hot, and there is no question why I'm on fire. But the instant thought of me being bare under my skirt is what flushes my cheeks in panic. *Why didn't I get panties the moment I got out of the hotel?* It completely slipped my mind.

I look left and right, and alarmed I try to get up but his other hand presses my shoulder firmly down, holding me in place.

"What is it, Eliza?" His eyes instantly lock mine, and as his hand slides up under my skirt, something carnal glints in his eyes. *He knows.* His nostrils flare, and his eyes close for a moment. He leans in closer, and whispers.

"Shh… You don't want the other people to find out, do you?"

I've stopped breathing, my eyes are open wide, and I shake my head as he locks my petrified eyes with a predatory smirk.

"Let's see what you have for me," his hand trails up to my hip, and his fingers spread over it. Then they trail over the top of my leg, over my pubic bone, and up to the other leg, and hip. I'm frozen in place, and most likely dying. But the torment doesn't stop. His fingers trace the line between my closed legs, methodically. He knows what's going to happen. I know what's going to happen.

My legs don't resist his unyielding, hot palm inserting itself between my inner thighs; they open voluntarily. It glides gently and slowly up to the apex of my legs, and down to my knees. Two, three times, maybe more. I stopped counting the moment my eyes closed, hoping, no, needing, impatiently imagining his touch right where he should have touched me in the first place. Where I want it most. But his hand never does. Just as he gets near, his index finger faintly brushes my pubic hair, stops, and as it retracts his thumb does the same from above - teasing me cruelly. This game he's playing is excruciating. My body aches, I'm deprived from what *he* instigated in the first place, and he... he's not even thinking of touching me *there*.

I try to straighten up on the seat, hoping he won't notice my legs opening more when my moment of salvation arrives. The pads of his fingers run over my skin, prompting me to slide down ever so gently, and into them.

"Give me your hand," he whispers in my ear.

"M-my hand?" It takes me a moment to process the thought.

An unexpected, round swerve with his fingers, suddenly lights me on fire. A spark. Or sparks. I moan and quickly cover my mouth. Luckily everyone is paying attention to the driver and most have their headset on.

"I want to show you something." His fingers continue to go down my slit, and then up, drawing together the fire coming out of me. He reaches the top, and, with his wet, slippery fingers he starts rubbing me softly, without any intention of stopping, causing a grand mayhem inside my head.

"W-what?"

"Are you questioning me?" His voice is calm, almost ominous. He lifts his left eyebrow just as his fingers pick up immense speed, undoubtedly opening a portal where debauched alter egos come from. My legs open more, and as a further assurance, Sean leans over me, covering me from the world. It takes me a while until my hand is under my skirt, and touching his.

His eyes are plundering my soul, and yet, appear so calm. He's fully under control as he takes my middle and index finger in his hand, and runs them up and down my slit, showing me the movement. All of a sudden his hand disappears, but our eyes remain locked as I start rubbing myself slowly, in circular motion, hoping my actions won't be detected by anyone. And if they are, I wouldn't care, not before I reach my orgasm.

My mouth is slightly open, I've stopped breathing, and my eyes are wantonly looking at him as my hips start to gently sway on the seat. I'm close, I'm burning, I feel the waves of pleasure arriving fast to my shore. The moment they reach it and come crashing, I cover my mouth so my moans can't be heard. A sudden sensation propels me straight to heaven, his fingers jerking into me hard, and I bury my head in his neck, stifling my moans against his skin, all the while riding my orgasmic waves to paradise.

Oh my God.

Coming back from my high, I don't move. I'm afraid to open my eyes. So I remain under his wing, nuzzled. Quiet.

"Hey, are you okay?"

I nod.

"Look at me," he pinches my chin gently and pulls me towards him. A kiss falls upon my eye lid. First one, then the other.

Languidly I open my eyes, I'm still seeing stars from the orgasmic rush, and it takes me a split of a second longer to see his face.

"Your wanton eyes are shameless, Eliza. I want to see more of that."

The bus stops in Kensington, outside Harrods, a large department store. The shrine of Princess Diana and Dodi Al Fayed is in the basement, which, although done in good spirit I've always found a bit tacky.

"The shrine to the eternal love of Dodi and Diana, in Harrods, the most famous of English department stores, owned by Al Fayed until six year ago, is a popular tourist attraction. The shrine consists of a fountain, two large portraits—one of Dodi and one of Diana—and floor-lamp-size candles, the scent of lilies in the air. Under a glass pyramid is a crystal glass from which one of them had drunk champagne in the Imperial Suite of the Ritz Hotel just before they died, and the so-called engagement ring, which Dodi had bought that afternoon at the jewellery shop down the street from the Ritz. Diana never wore it."

"Come, this is our stop."

"Here?" I hope we won't be going to Harrods.

"Yes, here."

Luckily, upon exiting the bus Sean takes my hand and heads in the opposite direction.

After a few minutes we reach Harvey Nicholls, another five-level department store. I've been in this part of London with my dad, and vividly remember looking at Hyde Park in the distance, desperate to go and see the great house located at the corner of it, Apsley House. I read that Queen Victoria gave it to Lord Wellington for defeating Napoleon at the battle of Waterloo. Unfortunately, at that time, I had no luck. It was all about dad and his work. Except when he took me to grandmamma's.

"I hope you are hungry." Passing the doorman, he leads me inside Harvey Nicholls, heading straight for the elevators. The sign is clearly visible, Harvey Nicholls Fifth Floor Restaurant. I'm not hungry at all, and I doubt Sean is but after the ride we had I need a drink.

"A little."

We stop in front of the elevators and I regard him quietly. I'm still amazed at the transformation from yesterday. His expensive tailored suit must be made for him. His eyes, as they swathe over me I see them glint, there is not an ounce of decency in them.

"Eliza, let's not forget to get you a few pairs of panties later on."

I blush the moment the metallic doors of the elevator 'ping' open. He takes my hand again and leads me inside it. It's only us in here and I turn to him, observing his face, my hands holding his firmly, as if my fear of flying has returned. I'm in a dream I never want to wake up from. He leans forward, pressing me with his body, and, with his mouth caresses my ear.

"You are beautiful," his soothing voice makes me tilt my head into his. My eyes close, and our cheeks touch softly. Yes, it's a dream.

Sadly, the elevator pings again and the doors open, making me stand up straight. It's the third floor, and another couple is heading to the restaurant. Sean wraps his hands around my waist and pulls me to him, my back to his front, giving them more space.

"E-Eliza? Is that you? Oh my God, I can't believe it! London is so small!"

I lift my eyes and crook my eyebrows. Olivia, the girl I met on the airplane is

135

standing in front of me with a tall, handsome man in tow.

"Olivia! Yes, London *is* small!"

I step forward to embrace her, hoping Sean would let me go but he's not. He steps with me, it must look like we are stuck together like Siamese twins. She hugs me awkwardly, and quickly pulls back.

"This is my cousin, Mateo. I told you about him, remember?"

"Of course, I do. Hi Mateo, nice to meet you. I'm Eliza. And this is Sean," I forcefully pull away from Sean while managing to look normal, and shake Mateo's hand.

"Buongiorno, Eliza. Sean." He shakes mine and then Sean's hand. His eyes haven't steered away from me.

"Where are you heading to?" Eliza asks excitedly.

"Fifth floor."

"That's where we are going! Do you have a reservation?"

"We don't need a reservation, we'll probably stay in the bar," I look at Sean for confirmation.

"Yes, probably," he states, warily looking at Mateo.

"We could join you for a drink if our table is not ready. What do you say, Mateo?"

Mateo has not taken his eyes off of me. He looks Italian; olive skin, dark eyes and dark curly hair. He is very handsome, but still, the attention I get from him is making me uncomfortable.

"Si, I would love to."

We reach the fifth floor and immediately we are met with hubbub of guests, waiting staff, and glasses clanking. The atmosphere on Saturday afternoon everywhere is the same. The bar is also brimming with people.

There is a table in the farthest corner of the bar, overlooking part of Hyde Park, and I see Sean heading towards it. Hopefully we'll get a sliver of calm amidst the clamor up here.

"Over there, Eliza," Sean offers me the corner seat, pointing to it.

I sit down but Mateo, without much thought, fills the chair next to me, a seat probably Sean meant for Olivia, and picks up the menu from the table oblivious to Sean's plan. Sean, clearly peeved, is staring at him with menace in his eyes.

"Mateo, our table is ready!" Olivia, still standing by the entrance of the bar, yells above the noise of the people. She had checked with the restaurant and seemingly decided to go directly to their table.

"Perche non... have lunch with us?" Mateo suddenly turns to Sean.

"Non questa volta. O mai." Sean coldly replies. Mateo appears stunned. He doesn't say a word. He just shakes his head and stands up.

Sean speaks Italian? Olivia has come closer now, unaware of what had just transpired between Sean and Mateo.

"Eliza, I still want to meet with you next week. You have my number, right?"

"No, I-I, um, lost my bag. I'll need your number again, please. I'm sorry."

"Sure thing. Make sure you say goodbye before you leave, I'll give it to you then."

She reaches for Mateo's arm and they head towards the restaurant, leaving us in the bar. Sean turns to me, the fire in his eyes still burning, and sits down in the chair.

"What did you tell him?"

"That he's not having lunch with you."

"Olivia - ,"

"I know her, she was flying with us yesterday."

"Yes, that was her. You did notice her. But there's no need to feel protective of me -,"

"What if she was involved in the kidnapping?" He interrupts me.

"W-why do you think that?"

"It's my job to think that."

"What should I do then? Not talk to anyone?"

"Correct. I'm here for the talking. And anything else you need."

"Sean, that's silly."

"Have I not given you everything you need so far?"

"Y-yes. Yes, you have." I frown. His demeanor is strange. I need him to be the nice Sean.

"Now, let's have a drink."

I nod.

"What do you want?"

"Gin and tonic, please."

As he is searching with his eyes for the waitress, I get up. He stands up after me instantly.

"I need the ladies room, Sean. I'll be back in a few minutes."

The walk toward the restroom feels like an eternity. With a packed room, I navigate through the people and tables as best as I can. Just as I'm about to reach it I glance back at Sean but I notice as he's talking to the waitress, he's focused on something on my left hand side, behind me. He glances a few times before his focus shifts fully.

I turn around and see Mateo right in front of me, with a drink in his hand and a handsome, genuine smile plastered on his face. What a coincidence. I awkwardly smile and step into the doorway of the restrooms, hoping to avoid even talking to him but my plan fails when Mateo steps closer.

"Sei una bella ragazza," he whispers with predatory eyes.

"Um, sorry, Mateo, but I-I don't understand Italian."

"I said, you are a beautiful girl."

"Um, thank you. I guess."

"Se non si vuole farsi male, lasciare ora!" I hear Sean's portentous voice behind me, said loud and clear. I turn around, confused at the tone he uses but the threat in his icy blue eyes is palpable.

"Qual è iltuo problema? Vuoi un po 'di me?" Mateo's angry too, that much I can tell.

"Sean, leave him alone. He was just being polite."

"Was he now?"

"You are being unreasonable. Mateo was -,"

"Get-inside-the-ladies-room."

Gently but firmly Sean touches my lower back, and pushes me out of the way and inside the ladies room. I follow his order, but only because I need the toilet. Not because he said I must do it. He will not decide for me now, or ever. Ugh! I disappear behind the door, leaving the two of them outside, staring at each other.

Two days ago I didn't think men would ever look at me twice, and now... Now it looks like I'm the only girl on this planet.

After five or so minutes I leave the restrooms and head for the bar.

Sean is not there, and glancing towards the restaurant, I see Olivia is sitting by herself too. Where did they go? I walk back to my table, and sit down. The drinks are not here yet. I look through the window, hoping to forget how upset I am when someone taps me on my shoulder.

I turn around and look up. Tourmaline-black eyes are staring down at me. The spade shaped dark beard and defined cheekbones are not so easy to forget. That's the man who hurt my knee before we boarded the airplane. He's frowning and smiling at the same time at me.

"Um, remember me? I was the one who...-"

"Hurt my knee! Yes, I do remember you."

"Yes, that was me. Listen, Ms..."

"It's Eliza."

"Eliza, I wanted to apologize to you for my behavior, I often get nervous when I'm flying and ...-"

"I think I should be the one apologizing," I say half embarrassed.

"Yeah, well, I did hurt you."

"That's correct, but - ,"

"And I would love to buy you a drink. If you are free, of course."

I look around for any sign of Sean, but he's not anywhere to be seen.

"Actually, you know what, sure. Why not."

I was going to have a drink anyway.

"I'm Kyle Augustus, by the way."

"Nice to meet you, Kyle. I'm Eliza Cruz."

"Would you like to join me at my table, Miss Cruz?" He gestures me towards another table, in the opposite corner of the bar.

I stand up and follow him. It serves Sean right for being an ass.

"Have a seat, I'll go and get someone's attention. What will you have?"

"Gin and tonic, please."

"Sure. How is your knee, by the way?"

"Good, thank you."

A waiter shows up from behind us and greets us with a smile.

"Mr. Augustus, good afternoon!"

"Good afternoon, Sasha. How are you?" Kyle sits down next to me.

"Very well, Mr. Augustus. I hope you are doing all right. What can I get you today?"

Kyle places his hand over mine on the table, which shocks me and I instantly pull back.

"Miss Cruz here would have gin and tonic, and I'll have a glass of wine, please, Sasha."

"Certainly," the waiter smiles and disappears.

"Where are you staying, Miss Cruz?" Kyle veers his body towards me fully.

"Um, King's Road."

"Are you alone?"

I smile uncomfortably. Sean said not to talk to strangers, but this man doesn't feel like a stranger. He was with us on the plane. He must have seen him as well.

"OH! I'm sorry, I thought you were flying on your own yesterday."

"I was."

"Right. I'm sorry. I apologize. I don't mean to be nosy."

The waiter is back within minutes. Wow. Great service in this part of the bar. He places the drinks on our table and disappears.

I grab my glass and take a long sip from my drink. I needed that. I look towards the table where Sean and I sat, he's still not back. With the straw still between my lips I crook my eyebrows at Kyle; he's staring at me weirdly.

"I'm sorry. It's just that, you look so much like someone I knew."

"Who do I look like?"

"Someone who's not with us anymore."

"Oh, I'm so sorry."

"No need to apologize, she lived two hundred years ago. It's almost as if you're her doppelganger. Very beautiful."

"Who was she? A family member?" Blood rushes to my face. He makes me feel extremely self-conscious.

"Sort of."

"What was she called?"

"Milli."

"My middle name is Milli!" I exclaim, and take another sip of the drink.

"Is it now?"

"Yes!"

"Tell me, what you do for living, Mill… Erm, Miss Cruz," he grins at his mistake.

"I'm still in college. What about you?"

"Me? I'm an inheritance solicitor. Or lawyer, as you Americans, say it."

"Inheritance solicitor?" I crook my eyebrows. *I can't believe my luck.*

"Yes."

"Wow. And what do you do as an inheritance solicitor?"

"We deal with disputes over Wills, Trusts and Probate, which often occur at times of emotional vulnerability and distress. Bringing such claims is especially demanding and can become acrimonious and fraught very quickly. So people seek expert advice to help resolve matters that are crucial and hopefully can potentially avoid litigation and costly court proceedings."

"Do you always talk like this? As if you are in a commercial?"

"What you must understand is that the spectrum of disputes is as varied as the families affected. We act for trustees, executors, personal representatives and for individuals claiming against estates, trustees or other parties. We also often advise on complex and cross-jurisdictional issues, and regularly work alongside other intermediaries based offshore."

He is precisely what I need for Monday. In case that big shot lawyer gives me a hard time.

"So you must be impartial to do your work, then."

"Absolutely."

"What about the people who pay you? That could make you biased."

"It all depends on what they want. If I'm fighting for my client to get a huge chunk of the estate then yes, but when working as an impartial party then of course, not."

"Still, you're threading on a fine line there."

"I am? How so?"

"It just that, I don't know, it seems that people rely on the lawyer's word a lot. And we all know how much that is worth."

"Please, darling, tell me. How much is a lawyer's word worth?" He's lowered the tone of his voice. I've irked him.

"As much as he gets paid."

"Have you ever heard of integrity, Eliza?" His eyes come alight with that spark lawyers have. It's what makes him attractive at this moment.

"I have. But equally, it could happen that at times you may appear partial to the others, and the system, when you perfectly well know you are not. Isn't that true?"

He closes his eyes to calm down, I think. His nostrils show his incensed state but within seconds, he's back in control. Appearing normal. *Is this how I look when someone annoys the hell out of me?*

"Truth can be many things, Eliza," his lips curl in a wry smile. "Like, right now, the reason you are asking these questions could be either that you were screwed by a solicitor in the past, and want to think that all of us are villains, or maybe it's because you want to be screwed by a solicitor sometime in the near future, and you're just trying your luck."

He holds my gaze firmly as my face is becoming crimson. I want to reply, but with my heart beat quickening and all this adrenaline in my blood, I'm not going to have a good come back.

"Yes, I thought so."

"Y-you are wrong," I lift my chin. There's something dark and foreboding in his eyes. He seemed pleasant a moment ago.

"Am I? I've never been wrong once in my life, Eliza. I'm afraid you'll have to be more convincing than that," his gaze is intense, making the muscles in my belly clench.

"The reason why I'm asking all these questions is the fact that... um, I may need your help, and I wanted to see how good you are."

"Did you now?"

"Yes, as a matter of fact." I'm trembling. I'd better leave. Now.

"Eliza Cruz," the tone of his voice has changed all together. There's fire in his eyes. He's looking at me with an odd smugness, I don't like it. "You tick all the boxes, and more."

"W-what do you mean?"

"It's time to go home, Milli." I hear as the bar starts spinning.

I try to get up, to move away from him, but all I can manage is move my limp hand an inch from him. *What's happening to me?* My eyes close; his breath, a warm gust of air on my ear, wine scented, is unsettling. "Shh... Don't fight it, darling."

"Ready for another chapter, Milli?" A soft, kind voice reached me. The latch got open, and that meant they were waiting.

"I have more questions for you," I whispered.

"Everything is in these books," he replied.

"Please..."

"Get down on all fours and show us your lovely bottom. Our cocks need a release," an impatient man with German accent yelled. "And where else should it be if not inside our Milli."

"Take it easy man," the kind voice growled at him. I couldn't see his face from where I was, only his feet. He was the one everyone called Ed.

I did what they asked me to do. I went down on all fours, and backed up until half of my body was out through that small door.

The previous morning I took my time. That's when the Luminary thought I should be reprimanded before I started with the reading. Five open palms slaps over my butt cheeks. It was excruciating. The day before, five men groped me. Everywhere except the place that needed it most.

And last night, last night left me with nauseating feeling in my body.

With longing.

With craving, and want.

No drugs, they said.

They gave me drugs, of that I am certain.

CHAPTER 8

I wake up in a strange position, restrained on a chair, my hands and legs tied, and my mouth taped. I moan through the tape. As the realization instantly settles in and terror like I've never known overwhelms me, I start to breathe gratingly through my nostrils. *They succeeded! They've kidnapped me!* In panic, my eyes open wide, where am I? The room is large, semi-dark, and as my eyes adjust to the light, in all my trepidation, I'm somewhat confused. I don't understand why I am here. This place looks like a mansion, not the stone cold confinement I expected to be taken to, on the way to enslavement. What I manage to see is pure opulence. Dark red curtains along the walls, dimmed red lighting and among the other smaller decorations and portraits, a large painting hanging right in front of me. A woman dressed in a stunning red ballroom dress. That's all I can see. Below the painting, there's a man sitting on red velvet arm chair. Upon seeing me he stands up, and saunters towards me.

I squint, hoping to get a better look. *Don't touch me!* I jerk my head away from his hand but he pinches my chin tightly and raises it. He wears a black mask over his eyes, but the moment I see those black-as-the-night eyes and a spade shaped beard, panic mounts in my eyes. With an abominable smirk on his face that makes me retch, he clears his throat before proclaiming loud in his English accent.

"My dear fellow members. I give you, Milli."

I tense as his voice reverberates through my body. There is a dead silence for a few seconds, just before the bright lights come on. *Oh god! There are so many people in here.* Suddenly all talking at once, men, all dressed the same and wearing black masks over their eyes, nodding and agreeing with him. Petrified, I have a feeling that my heart will fail me, and give in, but the instant course of adrenaline makes me pull on my restraints forcefully. *I'm getting out of here.*

"Now, now, Milli, where are your manners."

Vehemently I try to set myself free, I scream too, but my voice is muzzled under the tape. After a while of yelling, pulling and thrashing about, I stop. All that can be heard in this gigantic room is my heavy breathing.

"Kyle, perhaps you should let her speak?" Someone talks from the crowd. I can't see his face.

"We've found her. That's all that matters. And this time, things are different. We are not letting her go. Let her speak!" Another person calls out.

Kyle grabs my hair forcefully, and tilts my head back. I yelp at the burning pain shooting through my scalp.

"What do you say, Milli. Should we trust you?"

Quickly I blink a few times, and nod as well. I won't scream. Where I am, I can't see any windows. Nobody would hear me anyway.

Kyle Augustus removes the duct tape from my mouth heartlessly, and waits on me to say something. Or maybe cry, it was that painful. When no sound can be heard from me, not out loud at least, he proceeds to remove the ropes I'm bound with. *Could I get away?* I glance towards the exits in the room, there are two. One to my left, almost behind me, with at least twenty men between the door and me. And the other one is on my right, in the distance, through double doors, which are wide open into a grand foyer, black and white marble flooring and a winding staircase. This place looks like a huge mansion. That exit is not covered but it's pretty far from where I am.

The two men standing on each side of Kyle nod at each other, and approach me. Both are tall, with strong, broad shoulders and perfect skin. Under their masked eyes, I see devotion.

"Milli, I am Gio, and this here is Franco. It's a great honor to be the chosen ones for this task. Just relax and let us change you into something more suitable."

They help me up on my feet and, when I realize what their intentions are at the moment they start taking my clothes off, I push them away, start kicking and punching while holding on my garments for dear life. They don't fight back, Franco gently holds both of my wrists, and the other one, Gio, continues with his job. They don't care that I yell, scratch, kick and bite them, and pull their hair, too. I don't understand. They don't reciprocate. Just gradually, in their own time, manage to remove my clothes. One pulls my t-shirt off, while the other fumbles with my skirt.

"Kyle, she has a phone in her pocket!" Alarmed, Gio looks at Kyle for guidance.

Kyle takes the cell, looks at it comically, before throwing it in the bin.

"My dearest Milli. We live in the twenty first century. Where the hell did you get this piece of crap?"

"Kyle, look! Milli's naked. No underwear, or nothing!" Franco's discovery is met by a gasp from everyone, and... strange awe?

I can't breathe, my chest feel compressed, as if someone is repeatedly stabbing me with a sharp knife. I know mother would die if she sees me now. Disown me. Un-adopt me. Give me away. To these people, where I am. Maybe that's why I ended up here. I cover my body, my modest gem, and hope not to die of embarrassment. The only day in my entire life I chose to live my life, to be bolder, and this happens. As if they knew. Serves me right for being so trusting. Look where it got me. *Nothing ever comes out of trusting men.*

"That's the Milli we know. It's in your blood, our seductress. You can't fight it."

"What's in my blood?" I ask as I hysterically fight off Franco's and Gio's hands; I will not allow them to take my last piece of clothing, my bra, and let everyone see me naked. Regrettably, they succeed.

"What do you want from me??" I yell at the top of my lungs, covering my breasts and my sex as much as I can. Infuriated, I don't care if I die or not. "Someone, tell me?!"

"Quiet! Arms by your side!" Kyle bellows in his deep voice.

"Fuck you!" I spit on his face. My saliva dribbling down his mask.

"Hold her!" He sternly orders as he pulls out a silk handkerchief from his pocket, and wipes his face with it. Franco and Gio instantly grab hold of my arms and align them to my body, I'm naked in front of the fifty or so men in here when I'd rather be dead. Only, a tiny part of my raging fire inside me, disagrees. That part doesn't care if I'm naked or not.

"This is how we want you, Milli."

"My name is not Milli!!" I growl, and never stop trying to set myself free. "Can't you see? You've got the wrong girl! I'm Eliza! Eliza Cruz!"

Kyle comes closer to me, his scent reaching me first, then his frightening presence. He's tall, and intimidating. The mask adds an additional dread factor.

I look at him with narrowed eyes full of hatred when, unexpectedly and harshly he slaps the side of my breasts, alternating, first one then the other. Three, four, five, six times. I pull back, I struggle, I don't want him touching me but I'm held firmly in place by Franco and Gio's strong arms. He continues relentlessly until something snaps in my head, the madness I was riding on is no longer there. He stops too, and my open wide, muddled eyes meet his up close, before agonizingly he applies the most excruciating pain I've felt in my life. The cruel loud slaps directly over my nipples feel like I've entered the underworld, and when he pinches them with both hands, and tugs until I'm there, dancing with the devil, it hurt so much I begin to whine in pain. To plead with my cry.

"Yeeees, theeere you are. Welcome back, Milli. You'll do great after all."

My body bucks from the pain, his fingers release me and the men holding me prevent me from falling. Feeling destitute and overpowered, all I want is for someone to wake me up, and tell me all this is a dream. A nightmare that's going to end soon. But I'm still here, and living it. *He touched my body, and in front of all these people.* That's the thought that revives me again, after the shutdown. With my arms held tight, I lunge at him with my legs so hard that if I got his head he'd be a dead man now. And all this would end. Unfortunately for me Gio deflects my kick straightaway, and saves his life.

"Take her to the basement!" Kyle orders as he turns his back to me, and walks away.

I'm dragged away with the chilling exhilaration of the men around as I ruthlessly persist to kick my way out of it

162

They all follow us, up to the foyer with black and white flooring, and down the winding grand staircase, not one, but two levels below. I'm going down to my death. Straight to perdition inside this hell hole. Two floors below. Who built this mansion? And for what purpose? God, how many girls like me were brought here? I wish they'd open my body and harvest my organs for the black market. Anything but this.

The room they take me to looks nothing like a basement. It's spacious, and round, no corners in here. The ceilings are high, the lights lowered. The walls are covered again with heavy, thick red curtains, which begin to open slowly as we walk towards the center, revealing a dark glass wall. The ghastly contraption placed in the middle, on a platform, makes me sick. It's something I've never seen before, and yet, it's clear why it's there. The chair is promptly illuminated with a spotlight, making me squint for a second, it's too bright. Another set of lights come on but not in here, it's in the room on the other side of the glass wall where I see the outlines of everyone that followed us down below, quickly lining up behind the glass. Some standing, some pulling up chairs to sit down. *What the fuck...what the fuck...* The dark glass is actually a voyeuristic window.

"Why are you doing this? Can't you see you've made a mistake?" My voice is unsteady, the panic palpable.

"I'm afraid we haven't," Gio replies as he guides me up to the middle of the room, and places me on the wooden contraption with velvet padded seating on it.

"You have! I'm not whoever the fuck you think I am!"

"We know you are."

"I'm from Boston! Yes, my mother is English, but I was adopted in the States! You see? You can't have the right girl!"

"There is a proof that you are actually Milli," Franco says calmly.

"What proof? What proof?? Show me!"

"To start with, you look like her."

"Like who??"

"Second, you are feisty as her."

"Milli? Is that who you are talking about?"

"And thirdly, even talking to me, you are aroused," he points to my pebbled nipples.

"Wh-what?" I look at breasts, and frown. "You're stupid, you know? Can't you see I'm cold? So is that it? Is that all you have? Where's your real proof?"

"We have been searching for you for the past twenty years, Milli. We know the truth," Franco is losing his patience.

"Look, we all love you, Milli. Don't worry about anything. You'll have an amazing time with us." Gio has taken over, telling me things what nothing and nobody would make me understand. "Please don't reject us. From a small ten-member club, we've grown to a five hundred men stronghold. Money is coming from every direction. People want to be part of your legacy, Milli. And that's our aim. The Luminary is not sure how we'll proceed as five hundred men are hard to please, even for you, but he'll think of something."

"Wh-what do you mean five hundred men?" I nearly faint, blinking rapidly, rejecting the words I've heard. "Please understand you've got the wrong Milli!"

"We'll talk later, darling. Right now everyone's watching you," he points to the shaded glass walls around me. "The bidding has started."

The time stands still as I hear the man in front of me talk. No. I didn't hear that. It can't be.

"B-bidding for what?" I whisper as I look at the glass, and see the nightmarish silhouettes moving about.

"For you, Milli. We ought to get you a breeder tonight. Well, hopefully."

My eyes drop down to Gio, and I stare blankly at him.

"The man that will pay most for you tonight will be your breeder."

"M-my what?" I grimace disgust.

"Whoever will breed you, will help us get the next generation. The next Milli. And

166

you'll serve us better for that. We know you are a virgin, Milli. All we need now is someone to start you off."

"Oh my god," I whisper to myself, and almost fall down from the chair. It's only then that I realize my wrists are tied to the armrests, and my legs to the chair legs. I'm sitting on a velvet-padded chair with a large hole in the middle. But that does not worry me. It's the five hundred men and their intentions. *Breeder?* I doubt I have ever read of a word such as that. Spine-chilling.

"Don't worry. You won't be harmed. We love you, Milli," Franco smiles at me in an ominous way, and together with Gio, leaves the room.

I take a long deep breath, but somehow my chest is not big enough to take all this. I'm suffocating. *I'm not ready for this.* I try to blank my horrid thoughts, but I can't from the commotion outside.

They lock the door behind them. Two levels below the ground. They think I could run away?

Look after your innocence.

I'm asphyxiating in a room, imprisoned, restrained, to be sold as a sex slave. Not likely.

Men are evil, and they will use you.

Don't I know that now, mom.

You are in charge.

I have no control of my life. I'm a scared girl who's never been more alone in her life than right now. Maybe if I wasn't home schooled I could have found a way out of this.

I don't wait too long before the sound of the door being unlocked makes my heart jump, adrenaline shoots through my body, the horror in my bones makes me shiver. I look up at the glass wall, the light in the background has nothing on the dark silhouettes moving against it. But now they've stopped moving. As if the master puppeteer decided to take a break.

Someone opens the door, and enters. In the dim light I see a tall man, a silhouette, wearing a well-fitted, tailored suit, with prominent cufflinks, like everyone in here, and slowly walking towards me. I see him removing his eye mask; I don't know if I want to see who it is, or if I should shut my eyes deliberately and let them get on with it. Too late, my eyes have already adjusted.

The moment of eerie silence is broken in half by my gasp.

"Y-you?"

He rakes his hand through his pristine, smooth hair while I still hope I see an apparition. *No! Please!* I have a panic attack smothering me as he is getting closer, and my breathing is getting erratic. The moment our eyes lock, I see my fate written in stone. There's no running away from him. The architect of my demise.

"Shh," within a breathing distance of me, he presses my lips quiet with his index finger and then proceeds to tuck a loose strand of hair behind my ear. Tension coils in my muscles as I feel the back of his hand on my cheek, stroking me threateningly. "You are so beautiful, Milli," he whispers.

I open my mouth to say something, but all I do I stare in shock.

He has a glass of water in his hand, and reaches out to me.

"You must be thirsty," he says and forces me to drink, tipping it over in my mouth. I refuse it, push it away with my chin and the moment it spills over my body, the cold water wakes me up from the frozen state I'm in. Again my anger returns. Tenfold. I frown and I clench my jaw, the sound of my teeth gritting rings in my ears.

"Fuck you! Arghh! Fuck you! Let me go you asshole!"

I have never felt so much hatred for a living soul like I do now. I have no tears for him. Or anyone. I will survive. Out of contempt, I will survive.

He comes closer to me, his eyes darting from my eyes to my lips, and back again. He better not kiss me. I slant my head as if I'm getting away from his face and then come back with full force, head-butting him sideways as hard as I can. The thud I hear in my brain may have hurt me more than him as I hold tight and let the wave of pain wash over me. I glance at him and see blood gushing from his nose. In a split of a second he looks at the dark window, then back at me. Making sure everyone is watching, theatrically he gives them a bloody smile.

"She likes to play rough! Ha-ha! Don't we all?" He is holding his nose with his hand and, just like Kyle, he pulls out a silk handkerchief from his pocket and wipes himself clean as best as he can.

"You want it rough, baby? I promise you that's what you'll get."

A drop of warm liquid rolls down my forehead, probably his blood, and he wipes it away with his hand.

"My name is Sean Maximilian. But you may call me Sean if you wish," he winks. *Stupid Eliza! Stupid, stupid Eliza!* I feel nauseous, and I gag. Everything is connected. Kyle, Sean, the airplane, the kidnapping, trusting him. Last night.... *Everything.*

"Now, let's see what you are made of," he reaches out with his hand towards me.

I look away and hunch my back, pull inwards towards the chair, but it's futile. He pinches my breasts just like he did last night, except, last night I craved it and now... Now it sickens me! He rubs my pebbled nipples between his fingers for a while as I concentrate on rejecting the sensations and then proceeds to knead my breasts. Suddenly, he takes a step back and lifts my chin, searching for my eyes. After a moment of being unsuccessful, he slaps my cheek, and the other. Not painfully, but still, hard enough. Shocked, my eyes shoot directly to his, and we stare at each other when again, he slaps my cheek. Harder this time. Why does he do...? How is this possible? I'm immune to him. To everything he did to me, and now...

Again, he slaps me but this time I tug on the chains, incensed.

"Fuck you!"

"Or what? Tell me, Milli. What will you do if I slap you again?"

He pulls my chin to him, his eyes stripping my dignity down to the last layer and with his thumb he rubs my lips. I lunge at him with my teeth, I'm ready to bite his finger off but he's quick. He recovers it just in time. With half a smirk on his face, and flared nostrils his focus is now on my legs. He slaps my inner thigh harshly, and the other too. A few more times alternating as I'm jolting in the chair, each time at different place until most of my skin is red, and the pain is excruciating, unbearable.

My body is not listening to me anymore.

He stops, or so I think. I use the moment to inhale, to alleviate my pain, but suddenly he slaps me one more time, slides his hand between my legs and having found my gem, rubs my nub for a second before plunging two fingers inside me. I shriek at the intensity. I'm disgusted by the debauched and illicit way he is treating me, and yet… I quiver under his touch. His fingers are out in a second, he lifts his arm high up, showing the glistening liquid to the people behind the glass. *I die*.

"I think we know who's in the lead, gentleman, don't you?" He roars.

"Until you find someone to match my bid, she's mine!" He smiles, licks every drop off of his fingers while looking at me, and leaves the room.

CHAPTER 9

I'm angry, helpless and… and roused. I have no tears. I'm past that emotion. *Men are evil, and they will use you.* Yes, Sean turned out to be exactly what my mother said.

The sound of the door unlocking doesn't make me blink. They may have cornered me into being a malleable doll to suit their desires, there's nothing else to be in here anyway, but I'm still alive. I'm not giving up that easy.

It's Franco and Gio. They are taking me somewhere. I look at the glass as they are uncuffing my hands, the men up there are leaving in orderly fashion, creating a long tail. Whatever was going on, it's finished now. Some of the men steal a glance in my direction. Judging by their sneers, I doubt anyone can see me really. Only that girl, Milli. She's the one everyone wants.

I'm not tied, just helped, and pulled up like a rag doll, taken up the staircase to the ground floor, where we were before. The dawn is set and I can see now where the real windows are, and some other cracks through the thick curtains from where natural light floods in.

The men congregate here, in what looks like a drawing room. Some are lounging around, some are peacefully watching me, some are playing cards, others reading. I'm without restraints, but even I know there's nowhere to run. Kyle is not here. Sean too.

I'm made to sit down on one of the soft chairs by Gio, who places a few books next to me, on the side table, presumably to read. Franco is talking to someone at the back. The atmosphere is very much… Homey. As if everyone is living in here. As if nothing has happened only minutes before, in their basement.

Push their buttons, see their limit.

Mother pops up in my head. Not repulsed by my nakedness but repeating some things from the past. Things I've forgotten. The advice she'd always give me when I'd met new friends. It was important that I'd done exactly what she asked back then.

Naked, bar the rebel on the inside, I stand up and start walking slowly around the room, observing what's around, looking probingly at the paintings and decorations. *Gathering information.* I notice that, even though some have their eyes trained on me, or my body, they don't approach. Or even flinch. I go to the wall, to the long dark red curtain and stop by the first painting. Then, without any rush I walk the perimeter of the room, absorbing everything around me until I come across a small and rather peculiar golden frame. It's not bigger than my hand. There is a letter of some sorts inside it, in French. Mom never really wanted me to learn French but I did try to teach myself. I try to read it, to sound it out, to see what it says when I notice the subdued hubbub has ceased, everyone has stopped whatever they were doing and are now looking at me.

Confused, I frown, and search with my eyes for Gio or Franco.

"You do realize that you are standing in front of her letter," Gio says from behind me. He must have been following me all this time.

"Whose letter?"

"Milli's letter. Your seven-time grand-grandmother. This is the request, or, as some call it, permission, for her female descendants to serve Marquis de Sade's followers."

I look back at the letter blankly, "But what if you really have the wrong girl?"

The palpable silence in the room is broken by a small explosion, and someone's shriek at the back of it. Out of nowhere a smoke is coming up to the ceiling, filling the room quickly. On the floor, among the people a trap door opens, and men dressed in black speedos come out of it, followed by three girls dressed in straps and leather. Suddenly everyone's forgotten about me and run towards the exit. Three men remove the golden frame from the wall, tuck it safely inside a small metal suitcase and, as if I'm not there, flee the room quickly. As if by protocol. A few have stopped by a cloakroom in the corner, have taken the coats and hopelessly try to extinguish the fire, which has now started engulfing everything in its path.

"Stay here, don't move!" Gio orders and runs towards the explosion.

"It's that rookie again, he doesn't know how to play with fire, for goodness sake! We'll all die because of him! Excuse me!" Someone rushes past me and curses.

I quickly pick up a coat from the floor and swiftly, looking left and right, I cover myself with it fully. People run away from the smoke, but I go towards it, and disappear behind the smoke curtain.

"Milli! Milli! Come back! Fuck, Leo will kill us! Where is Kyle? Oh god, Sean!" That's the last I hear before I find a door and disappear behind it.

I find myself in a metal cubicle, with another door leading out of it, which leads into a room with three doors. *This mansion is a puzzle!* Frantically I open the first door. Stone wall. Then, another stone wall. I sigh before I open the third one. Thankfully, that's the one that leads out. The cool breeze tells me so. I run alongside the long corridor and through the last door, which leads me directly on the parking lot. The dawn is breaking out and hazily shedding light over the twenty cars parked in here. I get inside the closest one, a Mini Cooper, which is also the smallest and looks easiest to drive, and search for the keys. I tug down the cover flap above the steering wheel and they fall straight into my lap. I'm running on adrenaline; my hands shake uncontrollably so I still my hand with the other in order to place the key in the ignition. Once in, I start it and with a screech I drive down the pathway and towards the gate. Most men are standing outside, looking at the fire engulfing the wing of the mansion, and having seen me now, with frenzied panic they try to stop me. I accelerate without caring if anyone is in my way. I've nothing to lose. I'll run them right over.

Beeping violently on my horn I slam through the main gate hoping it will break through. Again, I'm lucky, the gates crash open and my airbag doesn't deploy. Driving directly onto a busy road could be fatal but as if someone is looking after me, nobody is around, I focus on the driver, me, being the middle of the road. That's the key in driving on the left hand side of the road. I don't know where I am, but I sure as hell won't stop until I'm safe. My thoughts run a million miles per hour, the only safe place for me is the US Embassy, in London. It has to be. *I have nobody.* Olivia! *Mateo!*

But how the fuck do I get to London? Speeding dangerously through the narrow country roads I suddenly find myself on a high street. I ease off the accelerator, and I'm forced to stop at the traffic lights. There is only one car waiting patiently behind me as I wait for the green light. Thankfully, they are not after me. On my left, just by the grocery store, the barrier is open, and there is a parking lot behind it. A woman, dressed in a coat and overalls, sweeps the pavement. She's one of those workers that start early. In a last minute decision, I turn left, into it and wind my window down.

"Excuse me please, could you tell me how to get to central London from here?"

"London? Um, let me see what's the best way to get there," without any rush she pulls out her cell. After a few moments, she gives me a glimpse of the map on her screen. "We're now in Cobham. It'll take you an hour to get to central London. Down the A3, that will take you ...," her eyes go down to my buttoned up oversized coat, and my bare legs protruding in the slit at the front. "Is everything okay, dear? You're not hurt, are you?"

"No, I'm not. Thank you. I, um, actually need the US Embassy," I tell her, as if she knows where it is.

Immediately she fumbles with her cell and looks at me, "Once in central London, it's on the other side of Hyde Park, in Mayfair. Grosvenor Square."

"Thank you. I really appreciate it," I make a mental note of the address and quickly close the window.

Following the signs leading to the A3, I find the road and start driving like there is no tomorrow. There certainly won't be if they find me again.

"Prime her for me," I heard the Luminary order to his goons. Noj and Rodney were their names. I call them goons, but really, they were as good as gold with me.

They took me one level down, into a grandiose bathroom and removed my clothes. Men in here love me, apparently, and so many were present for my inauguration of bathing. Watching, observing. Perverts that needed to be locked up, if you ask me. After they were done with me, Noj and Rodney took off their clothes, too. I wasn't afraid. I only wondered what they had in mind for me. I had given up the custody of my body already. But they were powerless against my mind. Nobody could take that away.

I let them do to me whatever was necessary, without any fear. Noj and Rodney carefully helped me into the bath, and, having added sufficient amount of liquid soap on the large sponges, they started lathering my skin, scrubbing different parts of my body. I wondered if they'd join me but no, they stayed there, on the edge of the large bath. Meticulously, bit by bit, they were getting close to me down there, between my legs. Softly, gently, quietly, as it was all part of the cleansing ritual. Long and soft strokes with soap, then rinse off with water. And again. For an hour at least. Nothing sinister. But it was. They were making me hungry. Their bodies were a giveaway. I knew that. We all did. The men watching us had such filth on their mind, I needed to bath all my life to merely wash their eyes of my skin.

My body was giving in.

But the excruciating massage was over. I survived. I was helped out, and laid out on a lounger. Hot, with face crimson red, and unnerved. Charles Mingus was playing discreetly in the background, a tune saturated with lust and desire, which made me sweat even more. With a towel in their hands they started drying me, softly, again, patting the cloth gently over my skin. It took forever. They took turns, worked in unity on my body. *They were priming me.* And fuck was I primed. I caught a glimpse of myself in the mirror, I didn't recognize my wanton eyes staring back at me. And, for a fleeting moment only, a thought came to my mind, urging me to see how I could appreciate all this. How I could love it.

Their love for me was clear; their large members were touching my body in passing, big and hard. I remember closing my eyes to soothe my soul, to tell my body to be strong, when I sensed my cheek being softly stroked by a firm, velvety skin. *I had to be drugged.* But I didn't give in. Soon I would, though. How did I know that? When I felt something on my face for the second time, something rigid, I opened my mouth slightly. To inhale, of that I'm sure, but also, too replicate my body.

And when I could take it no more, I was ready. They knew it. I knew it.

They didn't dress me at all. Naked, they took me to him. To a dimly lit, vast room, with high ceilings and long heavy red curtains on its walls. The soft, almost unnoticeable music was still playing in the background. It was unnerving. It had the notion of my craving in its melody.

There were other men in here with black masks on, sitting along the walls on the elegant open armchairs with stylish carvings. The large painting of a half-naked woman lying on a bed of thorny roses was on the back wall. Funny, she reminded me of mother. But the sign underneath simply said, "Milli".

This room was created for her. For Me.

There were various contraptions all over. Some I could guess what they were for, but other must have come directly from torture rooms. *This was to be my life?* The cold shiver that ran down my spine had the answer. *Never.*

The Luminary was the only man whose face I could see. He wasn't afraid. He saw me and came closer, his pale blue eyes instantly spiked my face and body, it was clear how ravenous this sadistic animal was. So much vile dominance oozed from in his demeanor, I grimaced in disgust. He was sucking out everything that was good in me, and took it in his carnal fire pit, straight to hell.

Focus!

He was forty - something. Dark short hair. Impeccably shaven. Narrow face, cold. And daunting. Intimidating. Wearing a tightly fitted black suit. Like everyone else in here.

"Kneel," he ordered. "Sit back on your heels, open your legs."

I wasn't going to listen to him. Instead, I looked back at Noj and Rodney for guidance, or help, but found that no help was available. They took my arms, and guided my body firmly down, on my knees.

"We are not going to wait any longer," he said matter of fact. "See my fellow men behind me? They want you. And so do I. Every single part of you."

"But I-I'm not read - "

"See it as a helping hand to enter our world. After all, you are part of it. And it'd be a shame not to enjoy it," he was talking to me but his hand was on his crotch, he was unzipping his trousers.

My heart was beating in my ears, but my mind tried so hard to subdue the sound. *Facts, not emotions.*

"We worship you, my dearest Milli," he sinisterly smiled, and ordered to the man behind me. "Set her up."

CHAPTER 10

My life has become fucked up. Ugly fucked up. They thought I am her, Milli, and that's what's petrifying, they are convinced of the fact. Each time the thought crosses my mind my lips part, my breath hitches, a silent scream is burning my chest as I struggle to keep my eyes clear from tears. My chest constricts, my breathing becomes shallow, and simmering righteousness fills me. *I'm not her!* The fact that I'm adopted right now is what's keeping me sane.

"Be serious. Facts, not emotions."

After an hour or so of driving burdened with self-depreciating thoughts I reach central London. I'm trembling, miles away from the house I was kept in, and driving between the cars, mostly taxis on Whitehall, there's always a chance someone might be following me. Big Ben is behind me, showing seven thirty on a Sunday morning. *They better be open today.*

London looks like it never went to bed last night. Some people I see on the streets never went home after their night out. Still in their party clothes, sequins and mesh, with smeared make up, they drunkenly stumble about while waiting for their bus to arrive.

Having stopped at the traffic lights, a person standing on the edge of the pavement, looking at a map gets my attention. Observing my surroundings fearfully I unwind the window and with trembling voice I shout at him.

"E-excuse me, do you happen to know in which direction is Grosvenor Square?"

"Sure I know. It's where the US Embassy is," the man replies. *A fellow American!*

I smile, aware of the sudden influx of tears in my eyes.

"Grosvenor Square is in Mayfair, south of Oxford Street. Keep following the signs for Oxford Circus and you'll find it."

"Thank you."

"I'm heading to Stonehenge today. I have to reach Victoria Coach Station in twenty minutes."

The man is eager for conversation but the light turns green just in time, and I wave as I drive away.

Thirty minutes later I arrive at Grosvenor Square. I park the car outside the steps of the Embassy and with the last drops of adrenalin in my body, I walk to the door. It's closed, but I'm not deterred. I knock on it repeatedly, I bang on the window, I hear myself scream and… I cry. And I start all over again. Until someone come and take me away, I will not step down. At eight o'clock in the morning all I know is that I'm alone, and I'm cold.

The men from the club will soon find me. I have their car, so it's only a matter of time. I lean on the door and dismally slide down to the ground. I feel numb, I wasn't going to cry, but my eyes are bloodshot and tears have already blurred my vision. Nothing and nobody can stop them. I cry into my hands, sob until I have no air in my lungs. My chest hurts from the strain. *How did I end up here?*

Out of nowhere, a car stops in front of me with a screech. Petrified, and in panic, I stand up to run for my life, or hide until Monday comes when, as if someone was watching me from inside all this time, and saw me act like a terrified chicken, the door of the US Embassy opens. A sympathetic face, an older man, greets me and reaches out to me.

"Come, let's get you inside."

I glance back at the car, it's a false alarm; the woman that got out is not even looking at me, she's rushing to work, or elsewhere. I take the old man's hand, and walk a few steps before finally, on US soil, I break. Shattered, I fall on the floor, and start crying. The door behind me closes while I sob uncontrollably.

"What's your name, young girl?"

"E-Eliza Cruz. T-they took my passport... they- ," I stutter and sob. My hair is stuck on my teary face, I'm holding my stomach, I think I'm going to be sick.

"Who took your passport?"

I can't reply. I need to cry, to get the fear they installed out, through my tears. To expel all air from my lungs, and to forget.

"Here, drink this, it will calm you down."

He passes me a glass of water. I sit up, still sobbing and wipe the tears off my face. The glass is cold, the condensation formed on the outside is disguising the burst of bubbles fizzing on the surface.

"W-what is it?"

"It's only vitamin B, nothing else."

I drink the glass of fizzing water and take the hand he had reached out to me, to stand up. I do and immediately, he pulls up a chair for me.

"I called the Council General. He's on his way. Take this," he passes me a tissue for my nose.

"Thank you."

We hear someone outside buzzing through some security codes, and the door opens again.

"This better be good." A middle-aged man rushes inside. Dressed in suit trousers and a white blazer, he's staring at the old man with knitted eyebrows.

"Council General! Thank you for coming at such short notice."

There's a familiar person behind following him in his track. It's Mateo - he's staring at me, and frowning. His dark hair is bushy, he has a swollen black eye and a cut lip. "Eliza? Checosa... What's all this?"

"Do you know this woman, Mateo?"

"Yes, Council General, this is a friend of my cousin, Olivia. I met her yesterday, when... um, when I was involved in a fight with the FBI agent. You probably haven't read the report yet." Mateo speaks in perfect English.

"Because of her?"

"Absolutely not. Because of the asshole he was. Sir."

"Mateo, you were in a fight with an FBI agent, in London? Goddamn you and your hormones! I need my security agent to be level headed, not act like a teenager on raging hormones."

"Sir, if I may. I had a day off yesterday. I'm always level headed when I'm on duty. Sir."

The little old man clears his throat, and nods at my direction.

"I'll deal with you later. That report better be good."

"Eliza, has he hurt you? What happened?" Mateo is already ignoring his boss. He looks at my coat, and realizes I'm naked underneath. "Franculo!"

Mateo and his boss look at each other.

"Take her to my office. We need to find out what happened to her," the Council General orders.

Mateo helps me up and wraps his arm around my waist, pulling me to his body.

My head falls on his chest. Right now, he's all I have.

"I don't know where to start. Everything overlaps. I don't know who to trust anymore."

"You are in the Embassy of the United Stated of America. You are safe."

"That's what I thought when … when…" tears surge in my eyes, and I start shaking my head.

"It's okay. Eliza, mio caro, you are safe here, with me."

The Council General is sitting opposite while Mateo is next to me, holding my hand reassuringly.

"I don't know what's relevant anymore. The moment I got off the plane two days ago, people tried to kidnap me. That's when I met Sean. Sean O'Connell. Or Sean Maximilian. Whatever his name is. He saved me, not once, but twice. But then   "

196

"What did he do to you?" The Council General asks as Mateo clenches my hand tighter.

"Um... He... at first, he spoke to a man called Darby. Lieutenant Darby, from the Metropolitan Police. When he saved me for the second time, Sean took me to the police station, to give a statement. Gunshots were fired at my grandmother's place. The bullets must still be there, you can see for yourself. I... I don't know if all that was a setup, and if someone named Darby actually exists. It all looked very real to me."

"Do you know which police station you went to?"

"The one on Kings Road. In Chelsea."

"I see. Let me check my intel," the Council General stands up and nods at Mateo, who promptly follows him out.

"Stay here."

"Sure."

They leave me alone in the office and, just as I've calmed down a bit I spot a small sofa in the corner. I go over there, and lean on it.

I haven't slept for more than twenty-four hours, I'm exhausted. And sleeping in the US embassy seems like the safest place for me.

"Miss Cruz! Miss Eliza Cruz!" Someone is holding my shoulder, gently shaking me.

"Um, what? Why? Um.. I'm sorry, I must have fallen asleep," finally I'm awake, and see three men towering above me. Mateo, the Council General and the person holding my shoulder. Darby. *"You?"*

"You've been sleeping for four hours, Eliza," Mateo informs me.

"While you were sleeping we contacted Lieutenant Darby and he was more than willing to talk to us. He came, and explained everything." The Council General states.

"Explained?"

"Yes, he informed us that you are very important to his murder investigation."

"M-murder?"

"Yes, your grandmother, Miss Cruz," the Council General reminds me, as if I need any reminding.

"So it's definitely a murder, not an accident?"

"That's what we think," Darby replies.

"But what about the people who tried to kidnap me? Did you know that last night they succeeded?" My voice is wavering, deserting me, but nevertheless, I raise it. "I was drugged, taken to this... This Godforsaken place, stripped from my clothes... and...and your friend, Sean, was there!!"

Mateo is looking at me with eyes wide open, as well as Darby.

"The guy who claimed to work for the FBI, the same person who was pretending to protect me, was part of the kidnapping gang!"

"It can't be! I've known Sean for some time now. That can't possibly be true." Darby defends him in front of the Council General.

"I saw him with my own eyes! I was there! I was there when he... when he…" I cover my mouth, and start sobbing into my hands, stifling my cries.

"Lo ucciderò!" Mateo growls something in Italian and embraces me.

There is some commotion outside the office door, and suddenly, it opens and someone rushes in.

"I came as soon as I heard!"

It's him! Sean! Instantly I push off Mateo and shoot to my feet, angrier than I've ever been before. I loathe him, it's nauseating, and feel utter shame at the same time. As soon as he sees me, he runs towards me. I don't wait, I lunge, punching his face dead on, and then kick his groin hard. He deflects my kick, and overpowers me by grabbing my hand and twisting it behind my back.

"You motherfucker! You… let me go!!"

"Thank God you're safe!" Sean exhales while still holding me strong.

"Let her go, you asshole!" Mateo runs to my help, but the Council General raises his hand and he stops.

"Fuck you! You're sick! You and everyone over there!" I struggle and kick against Sean's strength.

"You don't understand, I was there for *you*!"

"Oh, how convenient! How the fuck you knew where I was if you are not part of that gangbang!"

"Eliza, your cell! Why do you think you had it?"

"Why didn't you arrest them? All of them! You couldn't, that's why! Because you are one of them!" I scream.

"Stop hitting me, for fuck sake!" He shields another blow from me with his forearm. "I was going to! But I didn't want to blow my cover! If I'm going to do this properly, I need more time!"

"Arghhh! Time? If any of them had raped me it would have been too late!"

"They won't! I promise you, they won't! You're mine. They won't dare!"

"Mr. O'Connell. Lieutenant Darby. Word outside."

The Council General raises his hand again and instantly, Mateo is by my side, taking over from Sean and holding me from not digging his eyes out while the three of them leave the office to confer.

"Let me go, Mateo!"

"Okay, okay, mio caro, just calm down."

"I won't calm down, I'm going to kill him!"

"Did he hurt you?"

"Not as much as I'm going to hurt him!"

"Eliza, please, ease off. I'm only trying to do my job. Don't make it harder for me."

I take a deep breath, and raise both of my hands. "Fine."

He releases me fully, but doesn't let me out of his sight.

After an excruciating hour the Council General is back in the room with Sean. Darby's gone.

"Where is Lieutenant Darby?"

"This is an American matter, Eliza. It doesn't concern him."

"I think it does if my grandmother was murdered."

"In that case he will have to contact you separately."

"What do you mean?"

"Miss Cruz, the situation is more complicated than we initially thought so. Therefore, we'd like to give you two options."

"Two options? I don't understand."

"You could either go home now and forget this ever happened to you, or you could stay here and help us with the investigation." The Council General states.

"Wh-what the hell? You want *me* to help *you*? And who's going to help me? Are you forgetting, I was kidnapped last night, I ran away from there and…and look at me! Look! I'm naked under this coat! They nearly raped me! *He* nearly raped me! Someone should go there and burn that house to the ground!"

"I understand you might be stressed right now, but trust me, the situation is fully under control."

"I'm not going back to that place!"

"You won't. I promise you." Sean quickly retorts.

"After what you did to me, why should I help you? Fucking asshole!"

"Eliza, please. I didn't hurt you. I'd never hurt you. Trust me. I came back in the bar and you were gone. I had to find you. And I did, didn't I? Who do you think set up the diversion so you could run away?"

"Miss Cruz, these people appear to be enamored with you. We could use that to get to them. But don't worry. We won't allow for anything to happen to you."

I don't trust Sean. *I hate him!* He tainted me. I can't pretend *that* didn't happen. And I don't have a good feeling about this. I should go home now. I would, if we didn't need the money. *Damn money.*

"The only way I'll help you is if you let me have a meeting with my grandmother's lawyers, as planned."

"Done."

"To do that, I have to go to her house and note down the furniture in it. That was the whole reason why I came to England. The meeting is tomorrow."

"Let's not waste time then."

"Um, Council General, may I suggest something? Since my cousin, Olivia, and Eliza are friends, perhaps she could stay with me tonight, in my flat? She'll find something to wear, freshen up. I could also take her to her grandmother's house and deliver her at the lawyers first thing tomorrow."

"Absolutely no way!" Sean growls.

"Great idea, Mateo." The Council General smiles for the first time, fully ignoring Sean.

"Thank you."

"Eliza, you know you should be with me. I can take care of you." Sean is not giving up.

"Mr. O'Connell, you have no say in this."

"Shall we go?" Mateo offers me his arm. I clutch his bicep and try to avoid Sean's stare that's making me feel so guilty. Yesterday was great. There wasn't any other man for me but Sean. But the anger inside me is quick to remind me of the last twelve hours.

Maybe he did help me get away from that hellhole but there was something unsettling in his eyes last night. Something I've never seen before in anyone.

CHAPTER 11

Mateo had to call Darby last night. We had to have a police escort, he was afraid someone might be at grandmamma's house waiting for me. We stayed for four hours in the house, I don't remember working this fast and hard for anything in my life. I managed to note down in my notebook seventy-two items that seemed old and expensive. Still, there were small items that I ignored; I simply didn't have the time to go through everything.

Mom and dad sent me here for the money, and money is what I intend to bring home. We'll kick that cancer's ass and then I'll have her all for myself, to fight with, and hate and maybe *love?*

Mateo made me feel welcome in his flat. I don't know what I'd do if I hadn't met

Olivia on the plane. And she was so kind to me. She gave me clothes; a white t-shirt, panties of course, and denim skirt to wear. Lucky for me we have the same shoe size so I ended up with her Nike flats too. I owe them both big time.

They also lent me some money and gave me a cell. The one Mateo got for her.

"Sean will pick you up when you're done with the solicitors," Mateo was preparing me for the day ahead.

"What about my passport?" I asked him. I don't want to stay in England.

"Your passport was in the house they took you to, in Cobham. Sean saw it. He should get it back by tonight. That's what he said."

"And you trust him?"

"Mio caro, you know I don't. But the Council General does, and, well, it's my job to do as he says."

"I understand. Thank you Mateo, for everything."

"Maybe when all this is over you and I can, you know, go out?"

"Maybe," I smiled. He deserved that much.

With a Starbucks latte in one hand and my bag in the other, carrying the most important item in my life right now, my notebook, I'm standing outside the glass building I saw on the photograph three days ago. Fitzgerald Solicitors. The reflection I see of me in the glass highlights my large notebook, so I move it to under my arm. I hope I don't have to talk a lot. I don't have the energy or strength.

I push the heavy door, and immediately, I'm greeted by a receptionist with a frigid smile.

"Good morning, I'm here to see Mr. Leopold Fitzgerald. I have a meeting with him at ten."

"And you are?"

"Eliza Cruz."

"Yes. We've been expecting you, Miss Cruz. Please, go through. Third floor, once you get there, it's the first door on your left," she says as she walks me through the hallway and up to the elevators. Then she presses the button for the elevator, and it instantly opens for me.

"Thank you."

I walk inside and I turn my back to the wide mirror, looking away from any image of myself that would make me contemplate my appearance, and inhale deeply. In less than five seconds the elevator pings and the doors open, waiting on me to make my move. I locate the first door on my left, and head to it directly. I knock and enter, without waiting for a reply.

A boardroom set up meeting greets me, with everyone sitting at the far end of the long table. My grandfather Edwin and another person are on one side, and a man with a bald spot, a little hunched, is sitting opposite them, I presume that's grandmamma's lawyer, with the empty seat next to him probably mine. Leopold Fitzgerald, the man that was too busy and important to reschedule this meeting, is sitting at the head of the table. Wearing an expensive and tailored grey suit, white shirt and a dark tie, he probably hopes to hide his age. His hair is grey, but too sleek and shiny for an old man.

The moment he sees me entering, he leans back in his chair, and glares at me, with his eyebrows knitted and lips in straight line.

"Ah, Lizzie, good morning." I hear Edwin's voice. I recognize him this time.

The hunched man has turned to me and immediately, he stands up and extends his hand.

"Miss Eliza Cruz, I presume. You've arrived. Mr. Powell, Ms. Evelyn Fitzroy's solicitor. I spoke to your father last week."

I was right, he is on my side.

"Nice to meet you Mr. Powell," I say quietly.

"Mr. Fitzgerald, I'd like you to meet my granddaughter, Eliza Milli Cruz. She came all the way from Boston for this meeting." Edwin introduces me, causing the hair on my back to prick by hearing my middle name. I'm going to hate it from now on, I know it.

The old man, Leopold Fitzgerald, clearly avoids eye contact with me. He places old style round spectacles on his face and starts scooping the papers in front of him, his eyes locked on the documents. "Well sit down Miss Cruz, I don't have all day for this."

I sit down and I place my notebook on the desk in front of me.

"What's this?" He asks exasperatingly.

"My notebook."

"What do you need a notebook for?"

"I thought…," I glance at Mr. Powell but he is all jittery, anxious at anything that Mr. Fitzgerald says. One glance at Edwin and his smug face makes me think this is all for show. Is it possible that I came all the way from Boston for this crap? The plane ticket wasn't cheap, you bastard! "Excuse me, if you don't mind me asking, what is this meeting about?"

"Don't you know Miss Cruz?" There's a condescending tone in his voice, as if he was waiting for this. *What the fuck is his problem?*

"I do, but you don't seem to know."

He seems taken aback by my retort. Mr. Powell quickly tries to save the day.

"Mr. Fitzgerald, I apologize, Miss Cruz is new, and she hasn't been briefed. As we all know, Ms. Fitzroy wanted an external body to overlook the execution of the will and …and…"

"Mr. Powell, I do know the reason why we are here. Grandmamma left a lot in her will, which Edwin here ungraciously wants half of."

"Lizzie, I can't ask for something that's already mine," Edwin intervenes.

"My name is Eliza. And no, half of that is not yours. You divorced grandmamma forty years ago. What makes you think she was accumulating wealth for you?"

"The fact that she didn't think I'd outlive her?" His cocky response annoys me more.

"Mr. Walker, that's enough. Your divorce was… forty years ago, you say?"

"Yes, it was. But I don't see how that's relevant," Edwin looks at the man sitting next to him, for support. That must be his lawyer.

"That's correct, it's not relevant." The man next to Edwin confirms.

"Is it not? I think that fact is relevant for so many reasons."

"If you look at the agreement - ,"

"I've seen the agreement, Mr. Walker! But ...dear me," the old man removes the round spectacles off of his face, tucks them neatly in his breast pocket and looks in the distance. "Forty years is a long time."

"Mr. Fitzgerald, why don't we proceed? Mr. Walker doesn't want much. Only certain things that were obtained while him and the deceased were together, while they were married."

"What things exactly, Mr. Russ?" Mr. Fitzgerald's interest has piqued.

"Some items of sentimental value. Nothing more," Edwin answers coyly.

"Mr. Powell?"

"Yes. Miss Cruz, do you have the list of items me and your father talked about?"

"Everything is in this notebook," I look at Mr. Fitzgerald. "I could make a photocopy for you, and erm, for everyone else, if you want."

Mr. Fitzgerald is observing me with a suspicious frown.

"Mr. Fitzgerald?" My lawyer is waiting for direction.

"Of course, yes. Proceed," Mr. Fitzgerald states all businesslike.

I glance at everyone as I get up. Edwin and his lawyer are patiently sitting down, while Mr. Powell, my lawyer, is one of those nervous people who have no idea of what they're doing. I don't know why they sent someone as inexperienced as him. And the old man, Mr. Fitzgerald, is watching me like a hawk. His straight posture is unnatural. He has his forearms on the table, fingers intertwined and no movement whatsoever.

"Do you have a photocopier in this office?"

"Over there, in the corner."

I pick up my notebook and take it with me. It takes me a few minutes before I figure out how it works. We had better copiers at my college, this one seems ancient.

"Miss Cruz, as I said before, I don't have all day," he raises his voice from the table, making sure I can hear him.

"Neither do I, Mr. Fitzgerald, and yet, my time is not paid, like yours is. I would suggest some leniency on your part," I snap. I've had it with men and their demands.

Edwin nudges his lawyer in the ribs as he watches my face with awe. "She has Evelyn's blood in her veins."

Mr. Fitzgerald narrows his eyes upon hearing Edwin talk, and clears his throat. He was about to retort but probably decided to keep it to himself.

Luckily, the photocopier connects and it starts printing. I pick up the copies it makes and I quickly go back to the table.

"Here it is, it's three pages each. I hope this is okay " I pass it around the table.

Everyone starts quickly scanning the document. After a while, Mr. Fitzgerald looks at me.

"You did this?"

"Yes."

"All by yourself?"

"Mhm."

"When did you do it?"

"Yesterday."

"This seems thorough."

"It is."

"How long did it take you?"

"Three - four hours."

"So you've been at your grandmother's house yesterday. For three to four hours." He glances at everyone at the table, leaving his eyes on Edwin a second too long. I don't understand why he's questioning me on what I've done.

"Exactly."

"Where did you stay last night, Miss Cruz?"

"Um… Excuse me, how's that relevant?" I lean in, regarding him coolly. After the weekend I had, I'm not ready to share personal information with anyone.

"Legal reasons. In case we need you. Tell me, is everything here?"

"No."

"Excuse me?" Edwin interferes, confused. "What do you mean?

"Mr. Walker, I'll be the one asking questions, thank you very much. Miss Cruz, what's missing?"

"One particular item that should have been there, it's not. I couldn't find it. It's noted down as G-plan credenza. Also, there other stuff I didn't have time to note down. But the credenza is the one that could possibly cost a fortune."

"How certain are you that an item is missing?"

"My mother gave me a note of everything that should be there. I lost it in... um, as I was travelling, but I clearly remember the piece of furniture from visiting my grandmamma before. It was a teak credenza."

"And you've seen this 'teak credenza' with your own eyes?"

"Yes, once. It was at my grandmamma's house."

He clears his throat again before speaking. Something must be stuck in there, he's been coughing a lot today. Or it could be old age.

"I'm trying to establish if your memory serves you right, Miss Cruz. How can you remember one furniture item among many? Tell me, how long ago was that?"

"It was six years ago. That was the furniture she was clearing out when I was there, and asked me to help her with it."

"I see. Mr. Russ, your paperwork please?"

Edwin's lawyer passes some documents to Mr. Fitzgerald.

"Yes, I see it here. Collectors have their eyes on this particular type of G-Plan."

I hear Edwin's quiet cursing.

"The item in questions is a credenza, and the most famous designer who worked for Gomme, this is the makers of G-Plan furniture, was LB Kofod-Larsen. He designed the G-Plan Danish range in the early to mid-sixties. Kofod-Larsen's furniture is printed with a gold embossed stamp bearing Kofod-Larsen's signature and the words 'G-Plan Danish design'. His pieces are rare, as they are significantly more expensive than other G-Plan furniture."

"Y-yes, I think that's the one. It had a gold embossed stamp in the back of one of the drawers. That one should sell for at least a grand."

"Mr. Fitzgerald, may I ask for continuation of this meeting? This item must be at Evelyn's house, I must check myself to make sure it hasn't been overlooked," Edwin interjects.

"I can assure you, I checked everywhere, Edwin."

"We cannot continue this meeting if we don't have all the items at hand," Mr. Fitzgerald confirms my fears.

"But it's not there!"

"Mr. Fitzgerald, is it possible that Miss Cruz decided to hide the item in question and sell it herself? This could be one of the most valuable items in the house."

"No! Is anyone listening to me?"

"Right. In that case let's not waste any more time. This meeting is adjourned until next Monday." Mr. Fitzgerald stands up and packs up his documents.

"Monday? I can't be here Monday!? I must go home!"

"You don't have to be present Miss Cruz if you don't want to. Now that you came, we could sort out everything for you. Just make sure you give legal property access to Edwin Walker."

I clench my jaw, I'm very close to exploding.

"To him?"

"Correct."

"Never!"

"If you are not going to be here, I'm afraid you'll have to, Miss Cruz."

"Edwin, I will not sign any legal property access to you. I came here for the money, and I will get it!" I say as I stand up and head for the door.

I was made to sit in front of a tall wooden pole, on my heels, with my legs spread open. Noj and Rodney worked in unison, they pressed my back flat on the mast, and took my hands behind me, bound them tightly with rope. Then they proceeded to tie my body, and to restrain my head too against the wooden pole. I couldn't move even if I wanted to.

The last thing they did I couldn't understand until later. They placed something metal over my mouth, I thought it would be to stop me from screaming, and muffle the sounds for that matter, but it was the mere opposite. It had a hole in the middle, and it was lined with rubber which I had to bite on to keep my mouth open. I didn't want it, of course, I struggled too but by then, I knew I was overpowered.

The devil raised his hand, and everyone got up from their chairs, and came closer.

I closed my eyes, and focused on facts. Not the emotions. I was struggling, I was failing, I was falling. Finally, I was no more.

One slapped my breasts, and my red engorged nipples, for what seemed like hours. Sideways, upwards, downwards, inwards. An older man would help him, and hold my breasts together as he'd strike them both at the same time with the short crop he brought to this… so called party. A small beastly item that made me flinch every time it landed on my inflamed and burning skin. Others used the inside of my thighs like a delicious ice cream. Two men on the floor, licked and sucked between my thighs, coming at times dangerously close to the apex between my legs, but never reaching it. Lord knows I hate to admit, but I tried jutting my hips forward, so their grating tongues would touch where I craved them most.

Someone behind me placed his hands on my waist. He held me firmly, and dug his fingers in my skin. Then he started massaging me with his thumbs, making rotating movements, which ended with an inflexible pressure on my sacrum. Those inconspicuous actions made me open my legs more, arch my back, as my behind perked into the wood. I knew I was drugged, and I knew was giving in.

And alas, the time had come for their leader to approach, for he was watching me all this time from distance. The men made way for him as he stepped closer, looking straight into my eyes. He had his pants unzipped, and he was stroking his large, veiny member with his hand.

"Say aaahh," he said and stuck his rigid dick inside my mouth. I gagged. I violently coughed. I tried to move away, but I had ten pairs of hands holding my head in place, as well as the restraint to the wooden mast. They all wanted to try me. But he had to start first.

He didn't care of the noise I made. He didn't care if I'd choke. He started slow and then picked up speed, getting faster each time. And at the end, which thankfully wasn't long, he made me swallow his semen. Blue semen, they said. Blue semen shouldn't be wasted, they said.

After that, he sat down, and watched everyone take their turn. They didn't let me come, though. But continued their torture by pinching my breasts, slapping my thighs, they made me... They made me want something. They made me feel ... addicted.

Something heavy was lingering in my body. Between my legs. All over.

And as much as I hated it, I needed it, badly.

CHAPTER 12

Maybe it's just me being unfortunate, and stupid, but the past few days have left turmoil in my life. I still haven't called mom or dad to tell them I'm here. That I've arrived safely. What am I to say? That Edwin's desire to eliminate me is clear? Dad warned me. But I knew it all along.

I practically ran out of Fitzgerald's Solicitors - it makes me sick to even think Edwin would be dealing with grandmamma's will. One thing I remember she asked us not to allow. As if she knew this is how it would end up.

And Sean was supposed to pick me up after my meeting. *Where was he?* Where is he now? Nowhere in sight. He's left me alone, and vulnerable. I know Mateo said I should trust him, that he would keep me safe, but after what happened yesterday, I couldn't lie to myself, he is not on my side, and never will be.

With the left over money I decide to take the subway to Sloane Square, and from there walk to grandmamma's house. Should I wait until next Monday? What if I'm kidnapped again? They would do it, I know they would. Cold shiver runs down my spine. *I'd be a sex slave for the rest of my life.* The thought gives me a panic attack, and I hurry, I need to go somewhere safe.

Forty minutes of suspiciously looking over my shoulder and being paranoid of someone following me, I arrive outside grandmamma's house. I remember her watching me from the first floor window, her bedroom, that day I came. She was fussing so much around me and she wouldn't hear of me going out at all, or anywhere. She wanted me all for herself, she said.

The door is still bolted, the yellow police line in front of the entrance tells me it's safe to enter. But I don't just do it directly, in broad daylight. I walk to Anna's house and as our properties border, I throw my notebook over her fence and into my grandmamma's garden, and then, I climb on top of it and jump inside too. The grass is overgrown, there are spider webs all over but it doesn't bother me. In silence I look at the house just to see if there is any movement inside. Nothing. Even the door leading to the garden is bolted. I walk quietly to the back door and raise my foot on the window ledge, and then I pull the window upwards hard. This particular sash window was broken when I visited, and grandmamma kept saying the handymen couldn't fix it. But as nobody knew it was open, she was fine about it. Funny how things work out. And now, I'm using it to get inside.

After successfully entering I still check, and stop every two or three steps in trepidation before, confident that I'm alone, I relax and sit on the sofa in the living room. I take a deep breath, and exhale fully. Only now do I notice some of the painting in grandmamma's house. The main theme is fire. Or burning. The colors are auburn, red, yellow, and more often there is a candle, an open fire or a burning item. Some paintings look nice, like the one with the old woman lying down with a burning candle next to her. She's not dead, but very much alive. The candle is in focus though. Some of the other paintings are eerie. I think those ones are going to sell for good money. I don't know anything about art but I know the uglier the painting the more expensive it is.

Edwin was certain that the G-plan credenza is still in the house, and now that I'm here, I'm going to double check that fact in case I've missed it. Mateo and Darby did rush me last night.

I start at the front door and slowly go along the left hand wall and in and out from every single room, until I reach the staircase. After doing a round of the ground floor perimeter, I can say with certainty that the credenza is not on the first floor. I suddenly get a flash back of a memory, grandmamma was clearing the credenza when I was here, and I helped her, too.

"What are you going to do with it, grandmamma?" I remember asking. There were loads of documents, books, and papers that she was clearing out of it.

Her answer is still a blur in my head. Or maybe she didn't reply to my question. There never was a talk of selling it, though.

I'm up on the second floor now and start walking along the left hand side wall, making sure I get in and out of every nook and cranny along the perimeter. But it's not long before I realize I'm back to where I started, at the second floor landing. I'm sure she wasn't going to sell it. Or use it. But it's not here. I sigh, inhaling deeply and as I exhale I hunch my back, droop my shoulders and tilt my head back. And then, I see it. A hatch to the attic. And I smile. I haven't been there yet. Maybe there's loads more stuff worth fortune in there.

After a good twenty minutes of searching throughout the house for a metal staircase or a pole I could reach the hatch with, I give up. Instead, I drag the single bed from the room closest to the landing and place it underneath the hatch, but of course, now I have to add more furniture to reach it.

Again, I go in search of more things to add on the bed and luckily I find an old, sturdy chair. I place it on top of the mattress, and try to wobble it. Not the safest thing around but it would do. I climb on top of it and fully stretch, I'm just about reach for the hatch but a glance down below me and seeing the staircase leading to the ground floor, makes my legs tremble. I look up quickly and focus on the hatch. I pull the tiny handle and the door slowly opens down, towards me.

There is a stepladder that could be yanked down. I pull it down half way, and carefully get off the chair, and then off the bed. Then I push the bed out of the way.

I reach the stepladder by jumping and as I grab it, and pull it, I open it fully.

"Ha!" I shriek, and startle myself from my own voice as it echoes throughout the house.

"I better go up."

I cautiously walk up the frail and rusty ladder, and as my head peaks into the attic the smell of mold engulfs me. It's dark in here, my eyes need a moment to adjust. Once they do, I realize the attic is jam-packed. There isn't a space to move.

I climb to the top, get off the ladder and onto the wooden boards, and reach for something that looks like a switch. I'm hoping that's the light, and it works. When the flickering light shines under the roof tiles, I smile. There is more stuff in here than all together below.

But everything is completely covered in dust. Dirt. Ugh. With my index finger and thumb I try to remove the sheet covering part of the items and I can't help but grimace. I cover my nose and mouth with the shirt I'm wearing. As I let the sheet fall down to the floor, dust particles saturate the air and I stop breathing, at least until the dirt settles. Then I begin to see chairs, tables, drawers, all stacked one on top of another. And at the very bottom, the G-plan credenza. My eyes open wide in excitement. This is worth at least a grand. I'm going to call Mr. Fitzgerald and tell him. *Ha!* Edwin wanted it for himself, selfish bastard!

I start removing the chairs, one by one. Then the table, and the other stuff piled on top until finally the credenza is free. That's $1.200 that would help mom for sure.

I quickly inspect it from outside, and then open the drawers and the doors of the credenza, making sure it's in good working order. Everything works perfectly well. The last drawer is lined with green felt, and as I open it quickly, a sparkle catches my eye from the back of the drawer. It's a small brooch. I pick it up and examine it; it has red stones lined like an open fire. *In line with the theme*. This must have been forgotten in here when grandmamma was cleaning it. I smile and fiddle with the clasp at the back, and once open I put it on my t-shirt. Something personal from my grandmamma.

Now I need to see how heavy the credenza is, and I try to move it. Nope. It won't budge even one inch.

I look around to see if there is anything else that was missed, or looks expensive, but fuck knows. I have no idea. I'll claim all of this with one line - everything in the attic is to be auctioned, too. Someone will have to come, check all this and take it down. I presume that would be Mr. Powell, from grandmamma's lawyers. They have to execute the will and they better get to it quickly. That's the next thing I have to organize. Mom needs the money.

I get down from the attic slowly; I don't bother to close it at all. There's no way I'm going to do the whole thing again. I go in the living room and pick up the phone, grandmamma's landline. Next to the phone is the number for information.

I dial and ask for the telephone number of Fitzgerald solicitors and I'm instantly put through to them. I ask the secretary to make a note of what I've found. I also tell her to call Mr. Powell, and Edwin and his lawyer too. She couldn't advise me when would be the best time to meet with all of them. I say I'll be back by four pm and that she should call everyone back to the office by that time. I want this over with. I want the furniture sold. I want the money. And most of all, I want to go back home. No more England. No more being afraid.

A sudden bang on the door makes me jump, and without waiting to see who it is, I drop the handset and hurry to the kitchen, and directly into the arms of a masked man who's probably been patiently waiting for me in here, and who's also startled by me.

"Eliza, are you there?" Sean is outside the bolted house. A déjà vu from two days ago.

"Seeaaannn, help meeee!" I yell at the top of my lungs and instantly I see the butt of the gun coming at me. I close my eyes in terror, feel the thud and hope I can bear it. The flash behind my eyes comes first, and it hurts, so much. I lose my balance, but he is not letting me go. Someone else grabs my feet and I'm taken in their arms outside through the kitchen door, through the garden and the back wall.

"Get away from me! I'm not her!" I scream as I'm thrown in the back of a van, the door shutting straightaway. My primal instinct kicks in, accompanied by adrenaline. I'm thrashing about, screaming, kicking the van hoping Sean or even Anna from next door would hear me.

The sound of gunfire makes me stop, one shot going through the metal frame of the van, entering the front, leaving a laser shaped trail of light and exiting through the back of the van.

"Sean!!" Undeterred I yell again at the top of my voice, and keep banging as the driver accelerates and drives off.

"Shut the fuck up, bitch! Nobody can hear you now so don't waste your energy! You'll need it!"

"Here, start reading." Ed passes me a large, very heavy book. Ed is the gentle one. His voice is kind. He makes sure I'm comfortable, before and after. *He could be my way out.* As for the book, I've stopped caring what I'm reading any more. It's just words. Words over words over words. How would the words help me submit?

"Yeah Ed, show that whore who owns her," I hear someone talking stridently, in a French accent. "It's my turn after."

"Then mine," a plummy voice follows.

"I'm next," someone else says.

"I can't wait until we can take her backside!" I hear a taut voice.

I shiver in dread. I'm still being kept in this doll's house, but that's going to change real soon. And when it does, they will do with me what they please. I'll be their sex slave.

Everything is about your perception, mother would say. They all want me. Not in a distasteful and seedy way, but in a genuinely I-am-in-love-with-you way. They fight over me like teenagers. I heard their arguments early this morning. They all want to dress me, eat with me, take walks with me, fuck me, and I believe them, they would, but one at a time. Unless I'm happy with two, or even three, they joked.

So far only one has been around me. Leo, the Luminary, and as he said, he can't wait to stick his *steel hammer* inside me. So he can breed me. Ugh. I hate the word. It makes me gag.

"Sweet," another person makes himself heard. "I love a good tight asshole."

"Yeah not before Leo takes her," the vile conversation continues.

Don't be bogged down by emotions.
Information is everything.

Mum's words, not mine. Maybe her way of
coping.

"No, you're wrong. It's actually, not before
she gives us a girl."

"Oh yes, after the birth, then we take her
asshole."

"Fuck, I can't wait. Do you think Leo is as
fertile as he says he is?"

"He's the Luminary. He made all this
happen. I mean, look how far we've come.
And from the next generation, our future
Milli will be a blue-blooded mistress. I
would say, don't doubt him."

"Fuck, whatever we'll do in those two years
when she'll be out with a child?"

"The previous Luminary hired cover. Seven
of the best whorehouses would bring their
girls each night of the week here. For two
whole years. Fuck, that sounds like good
times. But the thing was, not everyone

enjoyed them. They were in love with Milli, and wanted to be faithful. To be in her good graces."

Shiver runs down my body. *What if I die?* I don't have it in me. *I'd rather kill them.*

I do as I'm told, and immediately, as my bare bottom goes outside of the little window, I feel the cool breeze of the room. I look back and try to see through the hole. There are at least five pairs of shiny shoes, all standing around me.

"Come on Milli, we're waiting," I hear an impatient voice.

I start reading, and focus on the sound of my voice. I know the most they'd do is touch me in places I don't want them to, and avoid like the plague what I need most. They all want me to ride the sensation, but won't let me reach it. Apparently Milli wanted it like that. And what Milli wanted Milli got.

So Milli never got to come.

Ed gently pulls on my net camisole in hope to cover me, but it comes down to half of my bottom. And then, gradually, I feel everyone's warm hands on me, stroking me, kneading my breasts as they hang freely from my body, pinching my nipples, opening my butt cheeks, checking how much I have before giving in. I know they are all enthralled by my glistening folds, I hear their gasps, their moans. Yes, they have been glistening all this time. From being starved of desire. I feel their rigid cocks between my legs, on my skin, but only as a gentle touch. Everyone is ready to fuck me, and yet, nobody does. It's a game they all play so good. The game that makes me lose my mind.

But today, for the very first time, I feel someone's fingers going deep between my legs, and, gradually, up and down my slit. I glance through the small opening and see Ed's hand gesturing me to keep reading. I do, and desperately try to steady my unstable voice, so others don't notice. The amount of vibrations I feel has quadrupled as he reaches between my legs, and rubs my nub so quickly that my knees buckle. I almost faint from the rapturous feeling.

"Hey, stop hogging her, I want a part of her, too," someone complains, but Ed is not moving away. I peek in between paragraphs to see what he's doing. With his trousers undone, and cock out, he is stroking me with it gently. He pushes everyone back and positions himself between my legs. Then he lifts my camisole up to my waist, to give the others more of my skin to touch, and with his cock he's going up and down my slit. My juices gush, and he smears them all over my sex, growling in a low voice.

"Wh-what are you doing Ed?" I hear panic in someone's voice.

Ed is not listening. He grabs my hips and raises me, ready for penetration. I don't wait, I perk up for him so his cock slides right where I want it, where I wanted it for all this time, slowly stretching me. I moan loudly. I give in. Another moan frees me from the shackles they put me in.

I help him by moving my hips down on him and feel his girth widening the walls of my tight, once only-fucked pussy. I moan, I've stopped reading, I'm sprinting up the stairs to heaven, and notice everything becoming still outside of my doll house. Silence imbues the room, as if everyone is stunned and looking at Ed, and what he's doing. Only his long growls punctuate the air.

He's in to the hilt, and I know this is the start of my release. He slowly comes out, and then pounds me again, getting me used to his size. And then, all over again. He pulls out to the tip, leaving me gaping open, waiting for his deep and stretching thrust, and then he thrusts hard and fast into me. Over and over, holding me by my hips, he's pounding into me harder each time while I feel my insides combusting, producing a heat and fire that emanates straight from my loins.

He leans in and squeezes my breasts. First one, then the other, pinching my nipples. I sense his rigor as he picks up speed, and as I close my eyes I come so hard, I whine loud, so loud, Leo could probably hear me.

Ed growls as he pumps his sperm three or four times inside me, and pulling back, I feel his last ounce of warm liquid trickling down my lower back.

"Fucking asshole!" A slow, frustrated cuss comes out of someone, uneasy about what has just happened.

Thoroughly spent, and petrified, with trembling legs I quickly pull myself inside my dollhouse. *Is this it?* Will it be open house for everyone now?

"You came inside her!" The man yells in exasperation.

"Nonsense." Ed says calmly.

"I saw you!"

Instantly their dispute is punctured by distant footsteps, alarmingly coming near, and sharply stopping outside the room we're in. The doors open wide, the noise coming from the hinges tells me they could give in any time soon.

"It was not inside, that would be against protocol. Get your facts straight, Bob. Check her back if you don't trust me," Ed hasn't changed the tone of his voice. Calm, and fully under control.

"I know what I saw."

"What you saw was a man depraved of the woman he adores. I'd do anything for her, and you, Leo, are keeping her away from us. It's not on. This is wrong. I don't want her to suffer. I mean, I do, but on her terms. We all love her, do we not?"

I hear agreeing sounds in the room.

"All we ask is for you to take her in your room and breed her. Because you know what, Leo? I need her. And the rest of the men in this room need her, too. The waiting is killing us." He concludes his speech.

I wait.

Everybody does.

"Hm. Right. I suppose it makes sense. We did give her longer than necessary time to adjust, and she is still rejecting us."

"Exactly," Ed agrees with him.

"Tomorrow night, we start."

Everyone disperses with a hubbub, grotesquely thrilled that my time has come.

245

I've been strung out for two months straight. Finally, I got some peace in my head. But even so, I have twenty-four hours before it happens. Before I find a way to save myself.

"Can I have the book back, please?" Ed startles me. I thought he left with the others. I don't answer immediately. I need time. Time to think. "Milli? Are you okay?" Concerned, he kneels down and opens the latch to see me better. He peeks through, but I cover my face with my hands and turn my back to him. I hear him sitting down on the other side of my enclosure, with the latch still open so we could talk.

"I-I'm sorry. I truly am sorry, Milli. You were probably hoping Leo to take you first. But… But I wanted your experience to be different. Leo is… well, Leo is harsh. He would probably hurt you. And I don't want to see you hurt. You see, I do care for you, Milli. So much."

"No, you don't."

"I do. Why else did I do what I just did? I wanted you to focus better when the time comes. As I said, Leo is not as considerate as some of us."

"Why did you…You know. Why?"

"I figured I'm the youngest around here, and as such I hope I'd be allocated to you when the time comes."

"When the time comes?"

"As your husband."

I sigh in despair.

"Why are you doing all this?"

"We are in love with you, Milli. All of us. We'd kill each other for one moment with you. For a single smile."

"How long have you been part of this?"

"We are all new. When the new generation comes, new members are approached. There is a waiting list for the Gentleman's Club we're part of, if you didn't know."

"How can you love me when you haven't seen me before? You don't know who I am."

"I do. You are Milli. The descendant of Marie-Dorothée de Rousset. You are the one we love and adore. We don't mind sharing you and you don't mind serving us."

"I'm not going to serve you."

"That's what Milli usually says. And then, she ends up being the best woman on this world. She's wicked, smart, debauched, funny, sexy, hedonistic and best of all, riotous."

"Who told you all this?"

"There is a five hundred page book on you and your predecessors that we must read in order to understand you, and to get in."

"And you think a book will tell you what I am like?"

"See? That's the rebel inside you that makes you, you."

"Please, help me understand."

"I'm trying to explain to you."

"Do you know all this is illegal?"

"The chosen Luminary is usually chosen for the job he does. He assured us nothing we do here is illegal, as long as we have the letter."

"Do people know what you are doing in here?"

"Yes, they do. Many prefer to mind their own business. You'll be surprised when you find out how many of us are in high positions in the city."

"When would I find out?"

"After you've had your child, you'd come back here, and see us for who we really are."

"Why do you think I'm not going to run?"

"Because once you have a child, you won't have a choice."

"You'll take my child away?"

"If that's necessary."

"Ed."

His eyes glint like a teenage boy.

"Wow. You said my name…" he grins.

"What's your name?"

"It's Ed for the moment."

"Why did you lie to your boss?"

"I lied?"

"Come on, we are both adults. We know what happened. You came inside me."

Silence on the other side. *Yes, he did.*

"Don't say it like that, Milli."

"How should I say it then?"

"I was making love to you. I was trying to get you to like me. I know how frustrated you must have been feeling."

"I do like you, Ed."

"You do?" He sighs loudly, as if that was his life's goal.

"There is only one problem."

"What?"

"You do know how fertile we are."

"What do you mean?"

"I'm one as my predecessor, Milli, after all. And if you came inside me…"

More silence.

"Ed, if you care for me, let me out."

"How can I let you out? It's not only me, others want you too, Milli. It's not fair to them. They want to make love to you, too."

"And it's fair to me?"

Nothing comes from his side again.

"Ed, What… What if I get pregnant?"

He clears his throat and closes the latch. Then he stands up and leaves the room.

That was the last time Ed and I were alone. Of course, until we started playing family. Until I gave birth to my blue blooded daughter, Elizabeth.

CHAPTER 13

Trembling, and half dead, I'm back to the godforsaken place I ran away from. Back to the ghostly house where you step back in time, where the extravagant surroundings are just another illusion for a prison cell. *Sean knows where this is.* He should be looking for me. *Someone* must be looking for me!

Sitting restrained on a red velvet chair in a room I don't recognize, under what looks like a life size glass dome, I've given up. My throat hurts from screaming. I'm not her. Milli, or whoever they are looking for, is someone else. *I'm not her!*

I see the light entering through the tinted glass dome I'm placed under, it must be still daylight. *They have another one of these voyeuristic rooms?* I also see men outside standing ominously, watching over me like hawks. I doubt they'll slip up again. Running away from this place was pure luck. I'll never have the chance to do it again. The large dome I'm under is placed in the middle of an even larger room. Not a chance for escape.

Suddenly, something's happening at the main entrance, I see the men congregating in a hurry. *Are they running?* I yell to make myself heard, but realize quickly I'm in a sound proof room, whatever I say bounces back on to me. The only thing I hear is the sound of my breathing, reminding me where I am – caged, in Satan's hell.

I observe anxiously what's happening. The crowd splits in half, and makes way for someone walking firmly towards the doors of the dome I'm in. The doors are dark, probably glass, too, but fully tinted, and I cannot see anyone clearly now. A few other people follow closely behind.

And then, the lock and bolt unlatch, and the double doors open.

I'm looking directly at the people entering, the dome is not very big but even so at least ten people manage to get in and stand around me, their predatory eyes burning my skin. My heart beats fast, I'm terrified and becoming deaf because of the sudden pressure in my head. I'm expecting my first heart attack, soon. My heart is giving in. *I've tangled myself in a huge, bloodcurdling web, I'll never know what is real anymore.*

Sean? How can one man fool me so many times? He's not even looking at me. And…and…it can't be!

"What did you find, Miss Cruz?" The man standing in front of me talks, his icy words reach me loud and clear.

But suddenly, upon hearing *my name,* my jaw relaxes. My focus shifts from this wretched place.

"Y-you said my name," I whisper, "He knows my name! See? It's Eliza Cruz, assholes!" I yell and look at everyone. "I'm not who you think I am!"

The old style round spectacles are pulled out of his breast pocket, and placed on his face. He has not moved, or made any expression. His impassive face is instilling dread in my bones, and I'm right where I was, alone and petrified. Sean is now watching me like a hawk, his eyes hooded and speculative, his mouth a hard impassive line. Kyle is here too. His eyes are like the road to perdition, focused, and angry.

"Miss Cruz, when you found the credenza your grandfather was looking for, what did you find in it?"

"What the fuck is happening, someone tell me!"

"Never mind that," he sees the small brooch I'm wearing and takes a step closer to me. He reaches out and touches it gently with his hand. "Piece by piece, you'll come home to me," he whispers. Then he pulls it roughly, tearing my shirt.

He sneers as he places the brooch in his pocket.

"Miss Cruz, you may be confused about your identity."

"I-I'm not. I know who I am."

"Your grandmother was Evelyn Fitzroy, was she not?"

"You b..."

"And your mother is Elizabeth Fitzroy," impatiently he interrupts me.

"Yes but I..."

"Then there is no mistake. You are Milli," he reaches out with his hand and strokes my head, in a disturbing manner.

I jerk away from his touch. If my hands weren't tied I'd show him a thing or two about making a mistake. He's old; he won't be able to take it!

"But I'm adopted!! I can't possibly be her!" I yell in his face.

"I remember like it was yesterday. We were searching for your mother far and wide for twenty odd years, and just when we found her, she ran away, and disappeared. That is, until you popped on our radars. Really, it was you that we were after. It was your grandmother's doing, my Evie, all over again. Without our Milli, we couldn't continue what we started. What we were asked to do to you, on your descendant's behalf. It's only two of us left in here from that time."

"This group that you see are all new members," he gestures to everyone. "From the moment we found, and shortly after lost Elizabeth, we've been preparing. But this time it will be different. We are better organized. Supplied with the right tracking device so you'll never, ever, run away from here. From us."

"You can't keep me in here!! You got THE WRONG GIRL!"

"As a matter of fact, yes we can. True, maybe there are some issues on the lawfulness of the whole thing, but I'm sure, in no time we'll turn you into our lover and life partner. After that, you'd be a willing participant. Isn't that right, gentlemen?"

All of them nod and smile, except Sean and Kyle.

"Leopold, you must decide. You said my chances are high," Kyle is angrily looking at Mr. Fitzgerald.

"And they are."

"Were." Sean growls.

"Patience is everything in here. Without it, we won't have again what we used to have."

"You Yankees think you can go anywhere you want and fuck up whatever we have! I'm the chosen one, Sean. Accept it!" Kyle's face is red in anger.

"Have you noticed that Milli is a US citizen?"

"Even better. American chicks are nastier than the British ones," he mocks.

"Of course, and there's that little matter of the bidding, right?"

"Which I won!"

"Did you now? I'm not aware of it," Sean is deliberately peeving him. "In fact, Leopold has informed me that I'm the one who's won."

"Leo? Tell him. Tell him!" Confused, Kyle looks at Mr. Fitzgerald.

"Kyle, Sean's heart is in the right place. He doesn't want to only fuck her, but he genuinely cares for her wellbeing."

"And I don't?! Fucking old bastard! Who made you the leader? I say let's put it to the vote!"

"Kyle, who do you think supports this club financially? Do you think the money comes from the memberships fees? Lord Leopold Fitzgerald has invested all of his estate in this pleasurable endeavor. For you, for me, and everyone in here. If I were you I'd keep my mouth shut, you asshole!"

"I gave money, too! My bid…"

"You see, Kyle, your half a million bid was a joke. This house cannot be run on half a million pounds for a mere year. My twenty million bid on the other side, have an open arms momentum, a sort of, welcome to the family, touch." Sean calmly states.

"W-what? I-I didn't know we were going to go into the millionth mark!" Kyle is regarding Mr. Fitzgerald, who is looking at me as if he's hypnotized, staring sickeningly at my body.

"In the bidding war, one must always focus on the prize. I paid a bargain; she is worth so much more to me. You, clearly, didn't want to waste your money."

"B-But I found her! I brought her here! It was me!"

"All you did was share the same flight to London and injure her with your luggage. Oh and did I say tried to kidnap her and failed? You couldn't even do that properly."

"H-How do you know about the luggage?"

"I was there. I saw you. Amateurs. All of you. You want the job done, do it yourself!"

"Sean, you are the right person for Milli," Mr. Fitzgerald says while still engrossed with me.

"No! *I* want her!"

"It's not about wanting her; it's about having control. Sean Maximilian commands control over everyone in here."

"How do you know he is not an ex-boyfriend? He is from the States, right? Or someone who wants to fuck us all up? Or..."

"Kyle, I have had a lot of time to re-think the rules. This time, everything will be transparent. Everyone will be exposed. The breeder would do his job in front of the members. They need to know when the job is done, when Milli is primed. There won't be any more undisclosed conversations, or clandestine moments, which were exactly what took *my* Milli away back then. My Milli was amazing," Mr. Fitzgerald pauses, and strokes my head. "Your grandmother was the jewel in everyone's eye. But what she did hurt me so much. I loved her. We all did. And we genuinely thought she loved us, too. Boy was she clever."

"Why??" I ask with a grating voice, loud. The whole room hushes.

"Excuse me?"

"Why?" Dejected, but still not accepting my fate, tears fall down my eyes as I look at him. I may suffer the life of someone I'm not but I will not go down quietly.

Why?

"My dear, I don't think you've been properly familiarized with our club. Actually, this is more of your club. A club established two centuries ago, all thanks to your ancestor, Marie-Dorothée de Rousset, or, Milli. Her love for the Marquis de Sade was so great that she openly wanted for all

262

of her female descendants to experience what she had. So, this club was founded, and with the help of its affluent and wealthy members, it has been kept afloat until now. Her aim was to show you the life she had with the Marquis de Sade. The love, the pain, the pleasure. Altogether, in one."

"What you're doing is illegal! You hear me?"

"Trust me, soon, you will be the one who'll want to serve us."

I clench my jaw, grimace and shake my head. "Never!"

He smiles kindly, "My Milli was like you. Feisty."

"You're all assholes! If only one of you could hear me talk, you'd know that I AM NOT RELATED TO MILLI! I-AM-ADOPTED!"

"Eliza, you're not adopted," Sean's deep voice cuts through my body like a sword. My heart starts pounding faster than it already is as I look at his eyes. "Your mother didn't want you to feel connected to any of this for a reason. She's been through a lot. She never wanted this life for you. But you see, Milli, it can't be helped. This *is* you."

"A-and my dad?" I whisper.

"She met him in Boston, after you were born. I'm not sure he knows about all this. Otherwise he wouldn't have been so willing to send you back to us."

The sound cuts off in my head... I see a black veil silently floating above me, dwindling, and finally reaching me. It's excruciating, like a hundred minute needles going through my skin. Tattooing me with black sticky ink that can never be removed. It's everywhere; in my hair, on my face, stuck on my skin. Right at this moment, my world breaks apart. Not because of the daunting perverted thoughts of a hundred men would keep me awake at night years to come, but because what I felt for mom was utterly unfounded. She wanted me to run away from home. She wanted me to disappear and spend my whole life hating her. Anything but the life she had. *Has she been enslaved, too?* Dad would have never sent me here. Everything, every single thing I did wrong in the past six months has come back to haunt me right at this moment.

Regret, shame, guilt, remorse, etched deep under my skin.

"Enough about her, when can we start fucking her?" Kyle huffs through his teeth.

"It's called making love, and not before Sean breeds her."

The sound gradually comes back in the room in the form of a train hooting in the distance, faintly reaches my consciousness, and my voice fearfully stuttering is what I hear clearly.

"Wh-what?"

"Sean is the chosen one. He will be the one breeding you. That's how we'll get our next Milli. And once we do, we know you won't run away. Because this time, the rules have changed. Unlike before, *we* will be the ones keeping the baby. We'll look after it. Get her pliant. Ready. She won't know anything different when she comes of age. As for you, well, you will just serve us as needed. Until the time comes for you to retire."

My face distorts in disgust. This is too much. I gag from the bleak insight he's given me, but nothing comes up.

"So you… were you my grandmamma's…"

"I was," he lifts his chin proudly. "I loved that woman dearly."

"But that would mean that I'm… You will rape your own granddaughter?"

"Please don't make it sound seedy. It's not. We all love you, Milli. Get that in your head. And no one will rape you. It's called *making love*. However, I certainly won't make love to you! The breeder is always asked to leave when his Milli retires, to prevent him from incestuous relations. Of course, my Milli was clever, she fucked us up so badly we nearly lost everything. I had to stay until I got this up and running again. For a moment, twenty years ago, we got false hope that everything was fine but again, Evelyn outsmarted us. She helped your mother run away. Ever since, we've been looking for her. Imagine our surprise when we found you."

"She was your daughter, asshole."

"That's correct."

"*She* managed to run away. *I* will too!"

"That's where you are wrong, Milli. All this," he points to the dome, "Took me twenty years to build. For you - never to see the light of the day again. Trust me when I say it. Besides, your grandmother is dead now. The sooner you admit to yourself you are alone in this world of men, the better for you... and us."

Tears have been rolling down my cheeks for a while now. I clench my jaw and bite my cheeks from inside. I will not even whimper.

"Come on then, what are you waiting for?" Kyle looks at Sean, interrupting the old man.

The old man's face becomes impassive again.

"It's time. Sean, you know the rules. I trust you will enjoy her."

Sean is observing him darkly, he nod, his lips in straight line.

"Let's give them some space. Everyone, out."

The men in the room head out and start populating the outside glass of the dome, pressing their hands and noses against it, some drag old oak chairs closer to make themselves comfortable. The curtains open fully, congregating in layers by the door, delivering a clear view for everyone along the glass.

I'm left in the room with Sean, who has his back to me and is loosening up his tie. He takes off his suit jacket and places it neatly on the chair by the door. Then he walks up to me, and unties my wrists, and legs.

"Remove your clothes and lie face down," he's staring at me as he's taking off his cufflinks and folding his sleeves up to his elbows. Fearfully, I stand up and, appearing taller by being on the platform, I lift my chin. *I would die before give in.*

"Don't."

"Don't what!? Don't fight back? You out of everyone here know perfectly well I would."

"And you know perfectly well where that will take you. Back on the chair, restrained. Do you want to lose your virginity like that?"

268

"Is that what you intend to do now? Rape me?"

"I will make love to you, Eliz... Milli. Perhaps a tad forcefully, but nevertheless, it will be love."

"You make me sick!" Contorted in disgust, I spit at his face.

Not flinching, he wipes the spit with his hand.

"You didn't have any complaints a few nights ago," his face deadpan, as if he's talking for the sake of it. The way he is staring at me is petrifying. I know he can pounce on me at any time, they are all waiting on him to do it but I'm not scared. I'm ready.

"I would rather die before I let you do that."

"Do what?"

"Rape me."

"It's not rape. It's making love."

He takes a step closer - it's game time, but I don't miss a beat. I quickly move my hand aiming for his face. Anticipating my punch he grabs my balled fist, as well as the other hand as I try to hit him. Then he crosses my arms behind my back firmly while pulling my body flat against his, front to front. Yesterday's heavenly scent makes me gag today.

"Just play along," he whispers into my ear.

I pull back and regard him, confused. His eyes radiate coldness you'd see in a block of ice, his face is exasperated, mad.

"Fuck you, asshole!"

"You leave me no option!" he thunders. Releasing my hands he grabs my t-shirt by the seam, and rips it apart, making me yelp in shock. I frantically grab hold of the torn material and don't let go of it while he forcefully pulls my skirt down. Then he picks me up in his arms. I kick and scream at the top of my voice but my rebellion is short lived as he kicks the chair off the platform, and lays me face down on the floor.

"I said, take off your clothes and lie down! But did you listen? Oh no, you didn't!"

"Let-me-go!"

His knee is digging in my back, and his full weight over me almost crushes me. Then one by one, as he's lying over me he restrains my wrists and my ankles with magically produced cuffs, which seem to be on a pull out system coming from the floor.

"When will you start listening to me?"

"Never!" I pull on the chain, fight against it but I just hurt myself. Lying on the platform, I'm spread open, naked, bar my panties.

He leans down to my head and ominously draws my hair away from my face. Then he pulls my chin so I face the window around me and points with his finger at it. "On the other side of this glass are one hundred men, each and every one waiting to take their turn with you. Smile for them!"

I close my eyes in dread and immediately sense his breath on my face, mumbling quietly over my lips, "Play along or I cannot help you, Eliza." Instantly, his whisper turns to loud, theatrical statement. "Look at them, they are all hungry for you! For the next twenty years, you are going to be their mistress! Their love story! Their life!"

I'm resisting the urge to believe him, he fooled me before. What does he want to achieve? Fucking me? He had his chance already. *Unless he was preparing me for this.* I turn my face away from him and from the crowd, hoping to erase my surroundings. This is it, I'm tied, and I will probably be gang-raped by everyone out there, starting with Sean. Every day. All my life. Just like my mother was, and my grandmother. And every other female person in my distant family. I failed them all. I count the minutes before my soul dies as the sound of his ragged breathing forcefully rams into my horrified mind. Before he rapes me. Before they all do. He's beside me, rubbing both hands together. His firm touch on my back startles me, and I rattle the chains yet again, not ready to give up.

"Calm down, Milli. This will help you relax."

"Get your dirty hands off me you piece of shit!"

From the base of my spine his hands crudely glide up, applying pressure as he traces small circles around my shoulder blades. *Is he... massaging me?*

"Stop… stop it! I don't want you touching me at all!" Lying helpless and flat on the cold floor, I twist to get his hands off of me. I don't need anything from him.

He ignores me and continues to roughly manhandle me from my shoulders down to the back of my thighs. Hard, quick, firm. As if he is the one who's upset for doing this. His hands glide over my bottom a few times, and then, unexpectedly, he slides his hands between my thighs. Using firm strokes from the back of my knees along the inside of my thighs, and up to my apex, he finishes with a sharp slap over my bottom. I wince. *I hate him!* Why does he do this? He repeats - ten, twenty sharp slaps on my bottom and I have stopped counting. I'm jolted each time by the soft stroke, and then, the now painful smack. He's tricked me into vexingly awakening something inside me. In anticipation of his next move, my body begins to frustratingly throb. But nothing escapes my lips. Only my sharp inhale of air warns me of my yielding.

I know it's because I'm tied. If I weren't, he'd get what he deserves.

"These will have to go," I hear his voice as his hands coil around my panties and the sound of ripping slices through me like a blade.

"No!" I scream, I try to turn around, to save myself the embarrassment, tugging on the chains, yet again, stark naked. In my last crumb of hope I look back, tears pooling in my eyes.

"Sean, please… please, if you have even an ounce of decency inside you, don't do it. Listen to me, please. I-I I really like you. We could do this under different circumstances, not here, in front of everyone."

He is stroking my inner thighs while looking at me. I get to him, I know. The gleam in his ice-cold eyes changes. I only need to break through to his frozen soul.

"Look away, Milli, I'm not done," his wretched voice clearly states what's to come.

And, I finally give in. Silently I turn my head, my face is back on the floor, sobbing, and awaiting the penance my predecessor agreed for me.

His hands lie flat on my sacrum, and slide down to between my butt cheeks. He's deliberating. I don't move, or fight against the chains. *I don't care anymore.* I'm waiting for him to spread me open and give me hell.

"Milli, I don't want you like this, dead. You will turn around and show me your appreciation."

They can fuck me all they want but my attitude is what I'm keeping. I don't comment, ignore him as he unlocks the cuffs on my hands and legs and helps me turn on my back. I'm flaccid, if they want my body this is what they'll get.

Taking both my wrists in his hand he holds them above me, as he lies on top of me, nuzzling his face in my neck.

"Follow my lead and I'll get you out of here. I promise," his faint words are barely audible. He looks at me, then he looks at the darkened glass above us, smiles and kisses me. Not a small, insignificant kiss, but a deep, powerful one, the one that melts your reality away. His tongue is deep inside my mouth, weaving with mine, which, at first reluctantly but then willingly, is playing along. He pulls back, and breathlessly mumbles over my lips again.

275

"There are so many reasons why I'm on this side, and you on the other, but please, please trust me."

"If you try to do something, I will tie you again, and I *will* hurt you," he states loudly, for the public.

Then he kneels between my legs, and looks at me poignantly. Grey trousers, fitted white shirt with a few buttons undone, folded sleeves bursting at the seams, forearms with muscles that could take out a professional boxer, he is looking at me and unbuckling his belt. I hear his zipper opening and I dare not look at him down there. I'm afraid. I'm afraid he will use me. Mom warned me about men. She was right. And here I am, my life in the hands of hundreds.

We look into each other's eyes and without severing our connection, he glides his hands over my breasts. I close my eyes; his lips are on my neck, going up to the edge of my earlobe, kissing me gently. His fingers tangle in my hair, and he pulls me up to him, regarding me, absorbing every particle of my existence. *Milli's existence.*

"Trust me," he whispers again.

As if we are in a slow motion movie, he waits for me to part my mouth, and then he kisses me, our tongues entwining in an unhurried dance. He cups my breast in one hand and kneads it tenderly and then he squeezes my nipple, tugging it just a little, enough to arouse me. Still, my coherent mind cannot switch off the hundred men staring at us.

"Milli..." he says between kisses. "Make love to me."

If the only way out of this hellhole is by fucking Sean I would, willingly, but I have no guarantee. He would use me, and I would get lost in his world. I'm already debilitated by what he's done to me.

I move my head aside, but he doesn't let me switch off. He pinches my chin and pulls me to him again, while with the other hand he opens my legs slowly, and positions himself on top of me. His pants are unzipped; his large member is out, hard as a rock dangling between our bodies. Immersed in his cosmic blue eyes, being held between hope and despair, I'm at an impasse. I'm damned if I do and damned if I don't. Either way, I'm fucked a hundred times from here to hell.

"Are you still breathing, Milli?"

He lifts my legs and guides me to wrap them around his body, making my hips lift slightly, allowing him full access. I feel his hardness against my sticky folds, and having positioned himself, he holds his cock against my entrance, and slowly enters me. My body stupidly doesn't resist. I'm wet, and without much struggle he slides in, stretching my walls as he moves. I gasp, whimper, and hold on to him. Locked together, he places his elbows on each side of my head.

"I need you alive," he whispers in agony. "Can you at least pretend you're having a good time?"

I spew fire with my eyes while my tortured body is simmering under his kiln.

"Sacrifice your virginity willingly, and I'll set you free," he mumbles over my lips clandestinely.

I frown upon hearing his words. He promised he'd save me from here. Did he only want me pliable? Was that so I would do it willingly?

"I... I thought ...," I try struggling against this weight, losing my mind from my blood boiling inside me. *I believed him, for this?* He's staring at me, holding me firmly in place while he cunningly smirks, and starts with his thrusts; deep, painful, hard. Each time he pulls it out to the tip and in again, his rhythmical pounding gradually picking up speed, tipping me over into the madness zone. And while I try to set myself free unsuccessfully, I'm completely out of my mind, grunting while he slams into me, seemingly in anger but knowingly in desire, his groans becoming louder, and I feel as if our bodies are merging. My arms wrap around him for leverage, holding him tight, and with each hurried thrust he pounds me harder and deeper. I hate him, and yet, here he is fucking me into oblivion in front of all these men. What has he done to me? I want this, I want this so much! I feel an eruption coming.

"Eliza... Milli!" He buries his head into my neck and rams harder into me. I cannot stop my garbled, loud moans anymore, followed by his groans, and the faster our bodies collide, I feel the tide and ride the waves of my orgasm while he releases his spawn deep inside me. So deep, and so long, an infinite, inhibited connection is made.

Out of breath and panting, we remain in this position while the cheers from the other side of the window become louder, and reach us, crudely waking me from the obscene dream I was in.

"Well done, Sean. We'll give you a few minutes to clean yourself up," we hear a voice on the speaker. "Then, it's party time! I hope you have it in you to fuck her again, although I'm sure you'll have to wait for your turn for a good while. We'll keep her busy all night, I promise!"

Three months after the Luminary raped me, I became pregnant. As he predicted, Ed got allocated as my husband. From that moment up to the birth of my baby girl, he and I played a happy family.

We bought a house together, we cozied up in front of the fireplace on the cold nights, we went out on the weekends like any other couple would. We entertained at home, had dinner parties. True, only men would come to those, but still, I was a wife, a mother, and free for the next two years.

But they were right. Being pregnant meant I couldn't run. And after my baby would be born, I wouldn't imagine myself running. No mother would. So I had to do something else.

The due date for my baby girl came.

Everyone from the club was at the end of their nerves. They were excited for her. And me? I felt no mother should go through this. Giving birth to a baby for someone later to claim as their own. I'd lose her the moment I give birth.

Ed, or Edwin as I later found out, was smitten with me, I knew I had to use that.

The first cry of my baby made me well up instantly, I was sobbing like a child. The midwife gave her to me, but he took her, and held her ever so gently. There were tears rolling down his cheeks too. *He knew. I knew.* When he was passing her to me, I held her so carefully, afraid I might drop her. I looked at him, and smiled through my blurred vision.

"She's yours, Edwin."

"She's ours," he said.

"No. You are her father. She's yours."

He was afraid to even say it. He was afraid of the consequences. He made a mistake, a heavy burden to carry. A burden I was counting on.

In the months that followed, he was confused. He didn't know what to do. Instead of enjoying our little angel, he stayed away from us, alone, in the bedroom. But I needed him to do that. I needed him to go through the guilt, and remorse, and all the other feelings. I needed him to be in my shoes. How could anyone imprison my baby when she becomes of age? I'd allow it over my dead body.

And then, one day, he came out of our bedroom with bloodshot eyes. His look, determined. That's when I knew all this would stop with him. Milli would be no more.

Silently we looked at each other before I invited him to sit at the dining table.

"She will not go in there," he said resolutely.

I nodded.

"But - ,"

"Don't worry about me. If the circle ends with me, I'll be all right."

"What if Leo tries again?"

"Remember my appendix surgery last month? That was a hysterectomy. He can breed me all he wants, use me like a rag doll until I die. I won't be giving him a child. To him, or anyone. Fuck them."

"You are brave, Milli."

"My name is Evelyn. Remember that, Edwin. I'm Evelyn."

"Evelyn."

I knew everything would be okay from then on.

With Edwin's help we got Elizabeth adopted in America. I didn't want to know where, or who with. I just wanted to be out of her life. For I was her only connection that could lead her straight to her demise. I never counted on, twenty years later that she'd be fiercely looking for her birth parents.

She did, and so she found me. She found us.

Evil has yet again fallen down upon me, and no matter how much I wanted to stay away, I couldn't. Elizabeth was my baby, my family.

When I found out about her, they had had her for two years already. She was there, all alone, tied, raped, beaten. Oblivious to why all this has been happening to her. With Edwin's help, yet again, we managed to help her escape. But it was too late. She was weak, broken, and … carrying a child.

I tended to her in the weeks that followed, and told her why I gave her for adoption. The same reason she should go now, and stay away from England, forever. It broke me to say goodbye to my baby yet again, but it had to be done. This breeding must come to an end.

"Don't let them find you," I told her. "Don't let them find your baby. Promise me that."

She didn't say anything. Her world was shattered. She called her boyfriend from the States, and they disappeared. I told her to stay in touch. Not often though. Just enough to know that everything is fine.

That was the end.

Until five years ago, when my beautiful granddaughter Eliza showed up on my doorstep. Her father, oblivious of our curse, brought her straight into the wolves' den.

I cursed the day she entered England, and at the same time rejoiced it, for I held her in my arms for the very first time. A bitter sweet moment, one I was ready to fight for again.

Eliza my beautiful granddaughter is a rebel without a cause. Just like me.

Edwin promised me I'd see her again.

Once the cursed letter is burned, there won't be anything held against us.

CHAPTER 14

Our bodies are wrapped together, his head buried in my neck as flurries of butterflies in my stomach turn to maggots, hoping to poison me to death so I could avoid my fate. I gag, I want to get up, but Sean keeps me firmly in place as we listen to the sound of the curtains whirring around the dome closing off.

"Stay still," he whispers.

In a few seconds the whirring sounds ends and another humming sounds I didn't notice before, cuts off.

He lifts his head and locks me in his gaze. His face is sweaty, glistening, like mine. I don't move. The dread of what is to come makes me appreciate what I have right now, for it would be my last part in my life that I have covertly liked. I smile dolefully and run my fingers through his hair. If this is all I get before I die, I'll take it.

Seeing the mournful glint in my eyes, he takes my face with both his hands.

"Eliza, don't give up on me just yet, okay?"

"It's too late, Sean."

He gently pulls out of me, giving me an odd, unsettling feeling, and hurries to zip up his pants. Then he finds his coat and throws it over me.

"Quickly, we don't have much time," his hand reaches out to me. I wonder how far he'll go this time to prove he's on my side, that he will save me. There is no going back from this, I'm tainted. But with no time to spare, or to doubt him - he's the better of the two evils - I take his hand and get up on my feet.

"Come on, we have a window of twenty seconds. Follow me."

All of a sudden a thunderous explosion rumbles somewhere above us, and shakes the foundations of the building we're in.

"Dammit, we're too late!" Sean hurriedly huffs under his breath.

"What was that?"

Shrieks and panic reaches us, the smoke and debris fill the room outside, while the dome remains intact. A faint cracking sounds makes us glance at each other, we know we must move swiftly or else we'll end up sliced by the glass falling on top of us.

"Run!"

I take a few steps, but I don't have much strength. My energy is depleted, my legs have turned into jelly, I can't move that fast. On top of that, I'm barefoot, and the glass keeps falling, keeping no prisoners. My feet are bleeding.

Sean is by the door, six feet ahead. Upon seeing me, he steps back and reaches out with his hand. Our hands lock and he yanks me hard, hurtling me into his embrace as a large slab of glass falls right at the place I was standing, smashing into millions of pieces on the floor.

The door is locked but Sean seems determined. The world around us is collapsing while he picks the lock slowly and, finally opens it.

"You're bleeding!" He shouts after seeing my feet and without any questions he lifts me in his embrace. Then he kicks the door open and runs out carrying me. There is lots of smoke in the house, it's difficult to breathe or to see anything, and at the same time, my eyes sting so much.

"Hold your breath!"

Someone is calling Sean's name. I can't open my eyes, it hurts, but I hear a strong French accent.

"You got her?"

"Right here!"

"You sure that's her?"

"I just fucked her, of course I'm sure!"

"Allons! This way!"

Dear reader, you've reached the end of Milli. I'm currently writing the second book in the series and it won't be long before it comes out. I promise.

Please feel free to recommend Milli to your friends, and/or leave a review on Amazon.

About the Author

Alexandra is living in Epsom, Surrey with her husband, her two kids, and a puppy. She loves writing, drinking Champagne and of course, wearing high heels.

When she isn't glued to her trusty laptop creating magic, you can find her on any of the social media platforms.

Her Instagram account offers an insight into her private life.

Her Facebook, Goodreads and Twitter page have more information on her up-and-coming events and books.

But it's her Pinterest account that will give you the biggest understanding of what's really going on in her head.

Feel free to (virtually) follow her.

www.alexandraiff.com

Printed in Great Britain
by Amazon

36942610R00169